Instead of Skipping Stones
Part One of a revealing four-book Series titled,
I Guess I Just Wasn't Thinking

by W.K. "Jake" Wehrell

ISBN: 978-0-9987632-0-0 (print)
ISBN: 978-0-9987632-1-7 (e-book)
Library of Congress Control Number: 2017936006

This is a conceivable work of fiction, though characters, places, and
events may appear to be the product of detailed recollections. Any
resemblance to actual persons living or dead or events and activities
is difficult to avoid. For plausible deniability and because of an
embellishment or two, we'll call Roger Yahnke's life story a work of
fiction. See what you think.

About the Author

The author's head-shaking array of adult activities have resulted
in him appearing in three TV documentaries (including the
History Channel), his photo in weekly news magazines (including
Newsweek), being portrayed by Robert Downey Jr. in a 1990 movie,
and having residences everywhere from a bougainvillea-draped
cottage on the French Riviera to a bamboo cage in Laos. But that's
not important.

This book is dedicated to my savvy kids,
who in spite of my flagrant and prolonged absences,
have grown up to be loving and capable parents,
exceptional contributing citizens,
and unremittingly supportive of each other.
I would have to say,
all credit to their great mom.

Table of Contents

Prologue

To The Series

I GUESS I JUST WASN'T THINKING is a four-part first-person memoir; a gender-centric saga that rides the rails of high adventure while delivering the least expected, startling revelations. Be at Roger Yahnke's side as he struggles to conquer a life-altering deficiency. His head-shaking array of adult activities include a proud beginning as a Marine Corps carrier-based pilot, being hired by the CIA, flying covert missions for foreign governments. Desperately seeking his male birthright he finds himself in scarcely credible exploits, involved in daring, intimate, and occasionally illicit escapades.

Paramount in this tale are Roger's always fruitless (devastating) feminine encounters. He is consumed by the search for that one woman with the right chemistry to unlock his manhood. Every contemplated activity—besides its actual merit, is heavily weighted as to its likelihood of him discovering that one female partner. This singular motivation evokes a plight of skewed perceptions, flawed decisions and overly zealous undertakings. Although it well could—the import of the Series is not so much in the non-stop action, intriguing venues or colorful characters, as in the frank and intimate narrative of Roger's condition; its all-embracing mastery of him and the crushing embarrassment when he sees again the perplexion on the face of another untaken female partner. To the dismissal of all else he remains hopelessly fettered to the quest to find that one woman who must be out there. You will more than once find yourself on your heels, reeling after a wholly unanticipated turn of events. His story consummates with a shocking finality of staggering irony.

To Part One

Instead of Skipping Stones is an unlikely prelude to his future, scarcely credible, duplicitous global adventures. It is a warmly entertaining collection of innocent and endearing admissions; a freshly narrated pre-teen to adult memoir. As the reader you will be caught up in a succession of delicate then progressively more thought-provoking scenarios. You'll find it hard to resist the bonding, as Roger trusts you and is willing to confide in you and share with you his innermost hopes and fears. The end of each chapter will find you with a knowing smile or a tear in your eye; wincing at Roger's adolescent doubts, conclusions, best guess responses, and almost happenstance choice of a life's work. But stick with this harmless narrative. It's going somewhere! Part One is a necessary step, perhaps Roger's only chance to win your approval and maybe even a bit of affection, before a devastating impasse besets him and his actions appear non-defensible. Only in the last couple chapters will the dilemma that awaits him be revealed; one that will condemn him to a desperate lifetime quest.

CHAPTER ONE

Play Acting

Can't remember when I first felt the need to strike people as different—appear special; be someone who deserved a second glance. I *do* know it frequently caused me to be overly concerned with what kind of impression I was making on the new kid in class, my uncle, or even a complete stranger who happened to be observing me. Or why I felt (and continued to feel) driven to be someone or something other than I was; maybe because I was so small and not special at all. In any case it started early on.

Mom's birthday was coming up in a few days—December 15th. Can't say I remember much about last December, but from all the goings on now, I'd better remember this one. Everybody was listening to the news; the President made a speech to the whole nation, and the way most grown ups were acting since it happened (and even talking to us kids) it seemed like that thing at Pearl Harbor a week ago was just about going to change the world. Right now though—in my world, I knew that as a seven-year old, if I could have my own present for Mom, that would be something *she'd* remember. Mom and I had a closeness that my father and I would never have. I wanted to buy a really neat gift that would show her how much I loved her (and make her love and appreciate me even more). And if I could just get some transportation it would be easy, because I already knew what that gift would be. A week ago I had seen a pair of ladies' gloves in Woolworth's; finely stitched, tan stretch fabric, trimmed with dark brown leather. Even at my age I knew these were classy gloves and I wanted to see them on my mother. She deserved gloves like these. She was a special person; you could just tell— real pretty and real smart! She even way back then she went to college! A little college up in New York state. And based on the expressions on peoples' faces when they found out, it must have been a really good college. I think *"Vazzer"* or something like that. For a while she was the editor of the *Ridgewood News,* and two weeks ago they had a party for her when one of her short stories got published in the *Saturday Evening Post.* Everybody looked up to my mom and I guess for good reasons.

Three days before her birthday I asked her for a lift to town, telling her (in general terms) what my mission was. She guessed, was flattered and didn't turn me down. The streets were clean and the ride was upbeat—wasn't even embarrassed to be seen in our ugly green 38 Olds (that we'd gotten in the will when Mom's dad died). I felt noble. Mom knew I had saved up my own money and would soon be proud of me. With the two bucks I had made shoveling walks and my allowance, I had almost four dollars in my pocket! I was sure that would be enough.

It was only three miles to town—we were on Main Street and approaching Woolworth's before I knew it. Everything was going just fine. Mom found a parking place right in front of the entrance. She acted coy, checking her watch and asking how much time it would take. I was excited, proud of this grown-up thing I was doing. I knew it wasn't expected of kids my age. I popped out of the car visualizing the slender-fingered gloves somewhere inside, just waiting for me to snatch them up. Entering the store

I glanced back at Mom. She had a soft smile on her face and her eyes were shining.

Inside, things would not be so easy. While I was sure I had seen the gloves in this store, they were nowhere to be found. I ran up and down the worn wood aisles, searching the arrays of sweaters, socks, hats, and nail polish displays. I was sure I'd seen them in this store; lots of stuff, *but no gloves.* I began to panic. I had no alternative. It was the gloves or I just didn't know what. (It had never crossed my mind to think of a substitute gift.) I could picture the gloves on one of these counters. I was sure I'd seen them here. Heartsick, I did one last frantic tour of the store, only breaking to a walk when something caught my eye that could have been the gloves.

After much longer than I thought I would be in the store I had to admit it, *there were no such gloves in this Woolworth's.* Dismayed, I was now faced with coming up with another gift. With my three dollars and seventy-five cents clutched in one hand I examined possible replacements, but nothing seemed right. Quite by accident, I found myself in front of a long counter displaying kids' toys. On it (though it wasn't something I would have bought for myself) I spied a neat Lone Ranger pistol set. The holster was thick leather with real lamb's wool, and a big silver stud in the middle of it. It sure was handsome. But as I said, I wasn't big on guns and it was something I could easily live without.

While standing there I noticed that I was being observed by a tall well-dressed woman just down the counter; an attractive lady who I'd bet was accustomed to being noticed. She had an interesting sharp-featured face. An ashen complexion was strikingly contrasted by dark red lipstick and a short cut of jet-black hair. I felt a need to add to the impression I might be making—strike a chord within her; cause her to feel a concern for me. I commenced to "play-act," first looking wistfully at the pistol set marked at four dollars, then while still in her scrutiny, holding up my hand with the three wrinkled bills and the three quarters. I stared down at the insufficient funds as sadly as I could, then back up to the pistol set (as longingly as I could) with the four-dollar price tag. Out of the corner of my eye I could see she had observed my apparent dilemma and her sympathy had been duly aroused. Having achieved my goal, I was ready to get to the task at hand: Finalize my choice for Mom's gift.

Hesitating a moment, unsure of which direction to start out, I suddenly realized the tall woman was standing alongside me (above me). Next thing I knew the three bills were snatched from my hand, and she was adding one of her own. "Here, you poor little darling, you just take this as a gift from Lola." Unable to react, I watched—mouth open—as she gave the sum to the sales lady and with a disarming smile plunked the Lone Ranger pistol in my hand. I was dumbfounded. I had never considered such an outcome. And based on the convincing nature of my previous charade, I had no recourse but to accept the gift (and her hug) and show a combination of joy and disbelief (the latter being easy), while thanking her profusely for her kindness. And worse—as if she had just adopted me, she was going to escort me all the way to the sidewalk entrance.

There was a rushing noise in my ears and a sick feeling overtook me. Everything, my excitement about the gloves, my feeling of doing something good; *everything,* was over. I wanted to break away, run and hide; start the whole day over again. At the exit, she stooped and gave me one big reassuring smile (that I tried to return) and she was gone, and I was alone. I slunk across the sidewalk and towards the car, not daring to look up at my mother's face. There I was, bearing a Lone Ranger holster set in lieu of those sleek driving gloves. To this day it hurts me to imagine how letdown and disappointed my mother must have been, particularly in view of the buildup I had given this trip to town. There was no need to try to describe to her the gloves I *meant* to buy. I didn't buy them. And I didn't dare to explain the scenario inside the store. I was too ashamed of my own part in it. I hated myself and that tall woman who had messed me up.

I guess Mom decided that I was only a kid, and what more could she expect. Probably thought I couldn't resist the temptation. Maybe she even thought it was foolish for her to believe I'd be different than the other kids; capable of doing something so special. Unfortunately, this would not be the last time I would play-act—affect people's conclusions and actions and find myself creating increasingly serious responses and relationships.

CHAPTER TWO
A Lesson In Chivalry

It was a scorcher! The sun was doing a job on the Oldsmobile's already badly oxidized paint job and baking us inside. We were right smack on the main drag for the whole world and everyone we knew to see—covered with sweat, our hair plastered to our foreheads. Mom had said she'd only be a minute. In the meantime we were caged, and I—the oldest (almost nine), had been left in charge. My baby brother Hank was raising a ruckus, kicking and bouncing up and down all over the front seat. *God what a kid.* A few months ago, doing the same thing, he'd smashed the glass face of the dashboard clock. I thought for sure that one was going to end the "he can do no wrong" treatment he was always getting from Dad, but he survived it. My sister Laura on the back seat—God bless her, just kept sobbing, her pink cheeks a map of wet streaks. Mom's bound to be back any minute. "C'mon Laura, please."

I rolled the windows down a little further—as far as I thought I could without Hank being able to jam his head out sideways (and get it stuck again). It helped. Laura's sobbing was getting worse; in my opinion, unnecessarily loud (with scary choking sounds). There was no calming her. The now half-open windows had the advantage of allowing more air in, but they were also allowing more sounds out. And these mournful sounds were beginning to turn the heads of passers-by. Hank was down on the floor in a writhing ball. Laura was seated properly but looking like a poster for UNICEF.

It was then I spied the elderly lady stopped on the sidewalk; bent and fragile maybe, but certainly not timid looking. Under the brim of her hat I could make out her eyes—fixed on us. She looked like she could be nosy and I was right. Her thin legs were now carrying her towards our car. I did not have a good feeling about her approach. She arrived at the passenger-side window, which moments ago Hank had gotten ahold of with his teeth (the saliva still there to prove it). She tapped it with the pewter handle of her cane, motioning me to lower it. Even in this heat she was wearing a high-collared blouse and long-sleeved jacket, with one of those same big cameo broaches that Grandma Deedy always wore. She had figured it out without asking: *It was I who was left in charge.* She seemed most concerned about my sister, and if you could have seen the condition of Laura's face you would have understood why).

"Young man" she said—face and cane almost inside the car, "Take your handkerchief and clean your poor sister's face."

Of course I knew what handkerchiefs were. I'd seen them in the breast pockets of movie actors and in those thin gift boxes at Christmas. I couldn't feign complete ignorance, but I personally wasn't in the habit of carrying one. In fact, almost never having carried one and not wanting to divulge this now obvious breach—after some quick thinking I said, "I can't. My handkerchief is dirty."

She recoiled an inch then leaned back into the window, fixed me with a stern look, and said, "Young man, don't you know a gentleman always carries *two* handkerchiefs."

CHAPTER THREE

1944 and Celebrating Armistice Day

There was one unsettling (and unfortunately daily) household event, that although I didn't understand why, always made me feel uneasy—even fearful: *The evening news!* At six o'clock sharp every night, Mom and Dad would take their places on each side of our big mahogany radio cabinet. Why? Because this wasn't just the evening news, it was the *war* news, and it was evidently something all adults were supposed to listen to. It was rattled off in monotone spurts by a guy with a real deep voice. None of us kids were allowed to speak. Mom and Dad sat there, lips pursed, heads canted towards the cloth grill, poised to make sure they didn't miss a word. There were a lot of new military words—allies, axis, brigades, divisions, plus names of islands and foreign cities, and numbers and letters and abbreviations. And the worst thing; hearing about the *casualties*—the number of dead and wounded (which always elicited clucking sounds or head shakes from Mom and Dad). Dad had a pad and pencil, and sometimes after a particular announcement he would look up at Mom for an okay, and she'd motion for him to write it down. And then, most nights, when the news was over, they'd go to the phone and call Gramp, and I'd hear them mention at least one of my uncles.

There was always a lot of talk about "our boys." *Boys?* I never understood which boys were involved in this thing. All my uncles (grown men) were gone, but none of *my* friends or as best as I knew—any of the kids at the high school, had ever been called up. But that's what I kept hearing. The big question was "when would the *boys* be coming home?" and what could we do here on the "home front" (whatever that was) to help get them home. At least one of the neighbors thought she was doing her part to get the boys home. Couple days ago at Victor Longo's house, I saw his mother tossing up and catching a baseball-sized mass of "tin foil." Back then, chewing gum wasn't wrapped in plastic, it was wrapped in a piece of waxed paper backed with a thin piece of real metal foil, and this was the stuff you were supposed to save. You used your fingernails to separate the metal from the throwaway paper; then kept squeezing the metal pieces together till you got a softball-sized clump. As she held the heavy sphere out towards me, I remember her saying, "This ought to be enough to kill a Nipper" (which I recently learned meant a Japanese guy).

Today was going to be a national holiday—just for "our boys." There was going to be a parade in town, one in Hohokus, and one in Midland Park too. Almost everyone on our street had a flag stuck in one of those brackets you see mounted on the front door frame. The big homes had real flagpoles like at school, anchored in cement in the middle of their front lawn. Even besides all this, I knew it must really be a very special day, because it wasn't often that Dad made a point of talking to me (especially sitting me down to talk to). With a finger extended and in a serious— almost confidential tone, he went on about the significance of this special day; about my personal obligation as a citizen to salute the flag and remember Pearl Harbor, and to think about his own brothers "over there." He called it Armed Forces Day, but I'd heard Veteran's Day a couple times. Not sure what it really was called. (I'd noticed that frequently other people did not use the same terminology as my dad.) He said it was supposed to happen on this day in November each year.

I was a ready convert and set about searching for a way to demonstrate my newly found patriotism. I wanted to appear and act in such a manner that it would be obvious to anyone that this household understood the significance of Armed Forces Day. Last Halloween I had received an army uniform costume (which unfortunately still fit); an ugly brown colored (not green or olive) shirt and knickers, and a hat to go with it. On leave from the Army Uncle Bud had called the hat a "piss cutter." I don't have any idea what that meant, but Mom admonished him for using such language. In any case, I put on the uniform and it felt right. Over the pocket I pinned three striped ribbons that Uncle Jim had mailed me from New Guinea. Although it wasn't part of the uniform, I topped the outfit off with my yellow Cub Scout neckerchief.

Appropriately attired, I decided to go one step further. I'd make up a commemorative sign and place it on our front lawn by the sidewalk. This way, in case of my absence all passersby would still know this household was in full support of "our boys." I found a piece of cardboard and pondered an appropriate message. It was an old shoe box lid so I was going to have to make it a short message. I knew about the Army and Navy; had heard all about the sacrifice our soldiers and sailors were making. I wanted a message that would honor them both. I roughed in the spacing and then printed the words as neatly as I could: "Army and Sailors." I said it out loud. But even though I didn't know why, the words didn't seem to match. I wasn't happy with it, but in order not to miss any more display time I decided to just go with it. I put it out on the front lawn and sat down cross-legged on the grass right next to it (holding a small US flag). Spent the whole morning there, sometimes standing to salute when passing adults took notice and appeared impressed. (Especially if they complimented me on my patriotism). It would be quite a while before our boys actually did come home.

CHAPTER FOUR

A Proper Burial

I don't think Mom or Dad ever took us to a pet store. We never got to beg for one of those furry, floppy-eared puppies behind the glass, but it seems our house was never without a four-legged resident—usually a cat. Between friends and neighbors and our own discoveries, we were always adopting some big-eyed kitten. Best I can remember we always had at least one cat. Now I don't mean Persians or Siamese, I mean just accidents; splotchy ones and striped ones. That's the only brands we knew. As common as they were I always ended up loving each of them, even becoming their champion. I was especially attached to our current all black cat (that we aptly named "Blackie"). I think Blackie was a girl.

One morning Mom got a call from Mrs. Sauerdell who lived across the street and down two houses, and whose son Warren, while presently working in a shoe store was going to be an opera singer. (He didn't get to do it, but she said he had been invited to sing on the Ed Sullivan show.) Mrs. Sauerdell was telling Mom that *she had seen Blackie in the street.* That was not too unusual and was wondering why it deserved a phone call. Mom on the other hand looked worried, hung up and started towards the front door. I was surprised by her concern and followed her down the steps, across the lawn and to the curb. And sure enough there was Blackie in the middle of the street lying on her side. Not a place she'd take a nap. I called her name, hoping against hope. No movement. A realization of the worst possible explanation overtook me. Heart pounding, I stood above her. Her legs were positioned as if in mid stride. She didn't show any evidence of having been hit by a car, but I knew that must have been what happened. I stood up and remained still; an appropriate moment of silence, challenging any oncoming car to make me move. Without saying anything, Mom (brave Mom) scooped up Blackie and started towards our house.

Real tears welled in my eyes—giving proof to anyone who might be observing, the effect this loss was having on me and would surely have for the rest of my life. Mom laid Blackie on the front lawn and went back to the garage for something. I removed Blackie's turquoise vinyl collar and put it on my ankle where I made a silent vow that it would stay forever. I could just imagine—years from now when I would be in some other place in the world, people asking me about the strange ankle bracelet I wore. It would be my secret (and add to my mystique).

Mom returned with a cardboard box and a shovel, but I was not ready for it to end so quickly and in such a way. By now Rolly had joined us and was looking down at Blackie, with what I deemed to be sufficient concern and respect. Donnie soon arrived as well (although his demeanor indicated he did not initially understand the extent of this tragedy). To communicate the solemnity of the moment, I managed to appear as shaken as I truly should have been. By chance, Kenny and George Jeffery from just down the street saw the commotion and came on down. I was determined that Blackie would have a dignified burial, with as many as possible in attendance. My four friends now here being the minimum!

I outlined the plan: We'd bury Blackie in the "sand pit"— an abandoned, deep excavation about a half mile away (whose original creation and purpose was never explained to any of us). The pit was isolated in the middle of a mile square block of dense woods, with only one long and winding path leading in to it. Don't know how any heavy equipment ever got in there to dig it in the first place. Besides being the only place with slopes steep enough to sled, it served many a day as whatever exciting location we chose to imagine it to be (from a submarine to an arctic wasteland, to an alien planet). A quick trip to the attic and I was back out with an old settee cushion. It was perfect! Light blue satin with a gold fringe. I gently laid Blackie across it. My plan was that with me leading, we'd make a single-file silent procession to the sand pit and lay her to rest in a fitting location. I was in disbelief, when ready to start the march one of the Jeffery brothers just up and left, saying he had to do something or other. My look was enough to convince the other three they'd best stay.

Everything proceeded with the reverence I had hoped for. Under the noon sun and at the bottom of the pit we found a fitting site and dug a perfectly rectangular grave. So far everyone had been a respectful mourner and I was grateful for their behavior. Standing side by side at the edge of what would be Blackie's final resting place, ready to lower her in, we all heard the whistle. And sadly, there was only one guy we knew that could whistle like that—that loud, with two fingers in his mouth. *Spike! My worst nightmare.* We were in big trouble. None of us knew where Spike lived (certainly not in our neighborhood), but from time to time he would show up, bully us, and then be on his way. This unfortunately could be one of those times. In unison we swung our heads up to look at the figure standing silhouetted on the upper rim of the pit. He was motioning to several cohorts (not yet in view) to join him. Two or three more roughnecks soon appeared at his side. It was an ominous profile.

Pointing down at us Spike hollered, "Hey guys look at that. A dead cat!" With these words he and his gang came leaping, sliding, half-skiing, down the sloping embankment of the pit. I have no idea how old Spike was, but he was a teenager for sure. He was wearing an old gray tee shirt with the sleeves ripped off, and filthy dungarees (with a silver chain as a belt). He always wore the same hat—one of those black felt skull caps with the fold-up brim cut in triangles, and little badges pinned on it. Before any of us could move (not that moving was an option) he was standing tall, directly in front of me on the other side of the awaiting grave. I was worried, real worried.

And I was justified in being worried. Without a word—just a devilish grin I can visualize to this day, he reached over, snatched Blackie off the cushion *by her tail,* swung her a couple circles over his head, and threw her with a dust raising thud into the recently dug grave. He laughed. His friends laughed. It wasn't funny. None of my friends said anything. I didn't either. We went home. I wanted the best for Blackie, but when it came right down to it, I didn't defend her. I let her be defiled. I should have done something. It was an early showing of cowardice and I was not at all proud of myself.

CHAPTER FIVE
Still Can't Believe I Did This

I was born with an attraction for small compact metallic gadgets; ones that were shiny or smooth to the touch, and especially if they had parts that clicked and fit, or looked as if they were from some bigger more important mechanism. This wasn't exactly such a contrivance, but it sure was neat. I'd seen it in a felt-lined drawer in Dad's tool cabinet for some time. Well—no reason why, but in the cellar one Saturday morning (after my job shoveling ashes in the furnace room) Dad just up and gave it to me! No real use I could ever have for it; he must've known that. Maybe just another one of those "spur of the moment" things he occasionally did. Not sure if it was a loan or if it was something I was supposed to take with me into my adult years. In any case I was now the custodian of a case-hardened, nickel plated *Sargent Senior* padlock! After handing the lock to me, he held the key up—three inches in front of my nose, and warned me it was the only one he had for it. Whatever I would do *I must not lose the key!*

I loved how it felt in my hand; the weight of it and the hard edges. It was one of the most valuably dense items I had yet been given control of. I memorized the serial number engraved on the bottom. Couldn't wait to show it to Rolly (same age and next-door neighbor left) and Donnie (one-year younger next-door neighbor right), but was afraid they'd ask the obvious question:

Part One: Instead of Skipping Stones

What did a kid my age need a lock for? I'd have to be ready with an answer—some great way I was going to use it. Try as I might, I couldn't come up with a single credible application. The good news was, when I showed it to them they inspected it and handed it back without asking the dreaded question. They were as much in admiration of it as I was. Donnie carried it for a while, and then Rolly—who kept using the key (which I never took my eyes off) to lock and unlock it. One time he somehow got it locked while it was *open* with the curved top bar completely the wrong direction. We couldn't budge it. It wouldn't rotate to insert it back in the body of the lock. Fortunately, after ten minutes of working the key and pulling and pressing, we had it back in working order. Toted it with me most the week—made me feel powerful. The lock in my pocket was like a gun in a holster.

But big trouble! At the end of the week *the key was nowhere to be found!* Retraced two days' steps. Grilled Rolly and Donnie, looked everywhere, but the key was nowhere to be found. I remembered Dad's threatening warning and each night began spending the last thirty minutes before falling asleep, worrying about the forthcoming consequences. What on earth would he say (or *do*)? He'd told me. He'd told me *only one key!* I was sick. If he ever found out—which he surely would, I just didn't know what he'd do. How could I have let this happen?

When I look back at the decisions I made and actions I took, many of them cause me to shake my head. Some are more embarrassing than others. This is one of those where I just can't imagine what I must have been thinking. In one of my most shortsighted plans ever, I decided to do something that would make the loss of the key irrelevant: *I would render the lock materially dysfunctional.* Skipping along the sidewalk with my two friends I feigned an innocent activity of tossing it up and catching it, except every one or two tosses I would purposefully miss it, allowing it to strike the concrete walk. Twentieth try and still intact! More tosses. More misses. Tried tossing it higher. I was amazed at how it was holding together. Out of sight of my two friends, I wound up and flung it against the sidewalk with all my might! Like my previous attempts, this didn't work either. I could not spring it open. I had no choice but to hide it and pray Dad would never question me regards where it was or what use I had found for it.

Fate wasn't on my side. At breakfast about three weeks later Dad just looked up and said, "Roger, where's that lock?" His question caught me off guard. Mind a blank I was surprised to hear myself respond (lying) "Out in the garage somewhere." Probably used the garage location because it was further from where we were sitting than any other place I could think of and added the word "somewhere" to be able to explain away the time it took me to find it. Both fabrications designed to give me more time. But there was to be no postponing the retrieval.

"Go get it." Now I had a real problem—*two* problems: one not too bad, the other terrifying. First, it wasn't in the garage. It was actually upstairs in my closet. And second, when I did show up with it, it would be *without the key.* No choice—had to produce the lock. I went to the garage first. Spent as long as I could there then snuck up the back steps to my room. Knew right where it was and found it easily, but in view of what might soon transpire in the kitchen, tarried a few extra minutes. Coming down the stairs my heart almost stopped; for the first time I took note of how badly scarred it was (the results of my failed attempts on the sidewalks). It was covered with scrapes and gouges.

Shaking in my boots and with sweaty palms I put it down on the table in front of Dad. A two-second look and his head arched back (probably to refocus his unbelieving eyes on the extent of the defacement). Both hands came up off the table. An initial look of dismay and then mounting anger spread across his face. I stepped back, knowing this was not a good time to be within his arm's length. It was a "dressing down" that had me fearing for my life. I took it, constantly mindful of the perhaps sudden need to duck; ready to dodge a hard hand.

When it was over, there was no doubt that Dad had lost all confidence in me as being old enough to be the steward of anything. Lots of disgusting looks and tongue clucking. I was sorely embarrassed. When he'd said just about everything he could, he picked the lock up and left the room shaking his head, *without ever asking for the key!*

CHAPTER SIX
In His Hands

Mom had a sister—Aunt Betty, and she wasn't well. I don't know what she had, but I'd heard Mom say it was incurable. I know it at had to do with the bones getting really weak. I heard her say that if Aunt Betty stepped out of bed too hard she could break her leg. Of course they never talked to me about adults being sick. I just listened as hard as I could whenever I heard them lowering their voices in the next room.

Uncle John was a neat guy—always joking. In fact sometimes he acted downright silly. He'd even play on the floor with us kids. My cousin Johnny had a trunk full of miniature tanks and artillery pieces and little metal soldiers. The three of us had swell times on their living room floor, playing war, laying out our front lines and positioning our troops. We even created battlefield topography by forming wrinkles in the carpet to simulate ridges and valleys. And Uncle John, if he didn't actually play, would act like he was making an official news broadcast of how the war was going. I didn't know any other adults like Uncle John.

Despite what I thought, Dad wasn't too keen on Uncle John. To hear him talk, Uncle John didn't work very hard (or at least Dad didn't think too much of what he did). Once when I asked, he said Uncle John just had the gift of gab and was a "bell ringer." Mom corrected him: "A manufacturer's rep!" In any case Uncle John always had cases of brushes in the garage and gave us two or three each time we visited. I'm not sure Uncle John even had a job now, since they had moved up-state. They were living in a little town called Shushan—in a parsonage. That's the place where the minister and his family usually live. But in this case the church had gone out of business.

Uncle John called last night. I answered the phone and this time he didn't make any jokes, he just asked for Mom right off. Once on the phone she began shaking her head and glancing at Dad, and I knew it wasn't good news. When she hung up she told Dad that Aunt Betty had been taken to the hospital, and that John wasn't optimistic, and that we'd have to leave in the morning.

We were on the road early (to "beat the morning traffic.") They left Laura and Hank with the Fitzgeralds but chose to bring me along. It was a long trip and especially in our small car. The back seat was loaded with stuff and I was all jammed up against one side with my knees and feet squeezed together. And I wasn't anxious for us to arrive, being pretty sure I wouldn't be good at whatever things I would have to do or say. At least I would get to see Johnny, although I guessed there'd not be any soldiers or anything fun this time.

Almost there—passing through Shushan's historic covered bridge; Mom's favorite landmark. It was all wood and made a neat rattling sound as the tires went over the loose boards. It was called the Deer Kill Bridge, which seemed to me a cruel choice for a name. I felt better when Mom explained that "kill" was another word for "stream. At the edge of town we passed Carriage Mill—a business in a barn that looked like it was still building horse-drawn buggies. Dad and I had walked down to check it out one time. It had a neat oil and leather smell. Now past the only gas station in town—with the strangest looking pumps you could ever imagine. Each one had a square glass bowl on top and you could actually see the iced tea colored gas in it. Finally at the end of an unpaved sandy street, shaded by large trees, between two weeded lots was the small two-story white house I had remembered. You could look all the way through under the house. The bottom floor was held up by a big square piece of stone at each corner, leaving it to sag a bit in the middle. No sooner had we bumped over the ditch and pulled up onto the property (there was no garage or driveway) than Uncle John was out the door and on his way towards us.

"Ken, Gay, thanks for coming. Thank you so much. Betty is home and she'll be thrilled. She'll be so happy." Dad shook his hand, Mom gave him a hug, and we were all marching towards the door. *Oh no*—found out Johnny wasn't going to be here. He was up in Albany at some school science fair. Inside I lost no time in scurrying up the steps to his room, where I would sleep that night (and hide for now). It didn't last. I heard Mom call.

"Roger come down here. Aunt Betty wants to see you." Knew I had to go but wasn't good at these things and was pretty sure it was going to start off with one of those awkward mutual hugs. Mom and Dad and Uncle John were seated around her bed. She spoke:

"Roger you've grown a foot since I've seen you." I smiled knowing not only had I not grown a foot since I last saw her, I hadn't grown a foot period. I just hoped I would grow a foot *someday!* But I smiled. Half because I knew I should and half because even though it wasn't true, it was nice to think that at least somebody thought I was getting taller. The room was not well lit; only one small lamp on the nightstand. Aunt Betty didn't look good. Her arms were thin and her skin looked loose and pale. Surprised myself by giving her an acceptable (but cautious) hug. It was scary but I did it. Uncle John beamed during the encounter—pleased at a show of some vigor by his wife.

"Tell me Roger, how have you been?" Before answering I had time to think that I probably should have asked her how *she* had been. But then again, that would have been stupid. I'd best just answer.

"Fine Aunt Betty, fine." Fortunately, the necessity of my presence was short-lived and I was excused. Back up in Johnny's room I looked through his baseball cards and admired his baseball posters. Johnny was a good baseball player—a pitcher. He knew the won-loss records of just about every team in the majors. I played with his metal soldiers, but it wasn't much fun alone.

That evening Aunt Betty took a turn for the worse. I heard hushed but urgent conversations from down the hall, and then Uncle John was on the phone calling an ambulance. Next thing I knew everyone was leaving and I was alone. About two hours later Mom called and said Aunt Betty might be going to die; don't know why she called to tell me. She asked if I was all right, and to fix myself something from the fridge (although we had just eaten before they left). Alone in the house I began to feel uneasy, and fixing a snack at least served to take my mind off the situation. Sometime later—in bed trying my best to fall asleep, I heard a car door slam. No matter what the report I would be happy to have Mom and Dad and Uncle John back in the house. I got out of bed and took up a position halfway down the stairs—not sure what to expect.

Dad was speaking. "Yeah John, she's a fighter all right." And Uncle John agreed that *she was tough that was for sure*. Dad added that he thought she even looked stronger afterwards (though he was not convincing to me). Seems they decided this failing was a setback that could be expected under the circumstances. I felt relieved. Aunt Betty had made it through again. As I started up the stairs I heard Mom making one last comment. "John, I thought for sure we were going to lose her. We can just thank the Lord. He spared her."

We had just finished breakfast—to me a much too normal breakfast considering the events of last night, when the phone rang. I could see by Uncle John's expression and hear by the serious tone, that it wasn't good. In five minutes they were all out the door and I was alone again, worried because this time—from what I heard, Aunt Betty might be worsening. I had not yet been this close to a death, and it was a proximity I wasn't at all anxious for.

Mom called a little past noon. They still didn't know anything. And no, I didn't have any problems with getting lunch, or anything. But six-thirty now and not another call. Expected to get one about what to do for supper (even though I knew I could heat up some Dinty Moore stew from last night). Time was not going quickly. I didn't know much about tuning their old radio or any of the programs that would be on the air up here, so just waited—all alone in the creaking old house. At last, at quarter to eleven all three came in the door—slowly, heads bowed. No one needed to tell me what had happened. Mom spoke, "We can just thank the Lord, John. He's taken away her suffering."

CHAPTER SEVEN
My Christmas Morning Paper Route

Dad had been right; eleven years old might have been too young for the responsibilities of a paper route—especially a *morning* route. But I could do it in 50 minutes if I didn't waste time and took shortcuts over lawns (and didn't stop somewhere to thaw out). Once I did it in 40 minutes! And it shouldn't be that cold this morning, maybe thirty degrees. (But it was really warm in bed). The bent-up corners of cracked leather on my bicycle seat would be frozen stiff, meaning I'd have to pump standing up. Five-ten; the papers should be here any minute. Some mornings even though I hadn't heard the bundle smack the sidewalk, I'd know they were out there. *How?* Because believe it or not—still in my bedroom, I could smell the cigar smoke from the guy in the truck.

And guess what morning it was—*Christmas* morning! I was pretty sure Laura and Hank would be up and ready to attack the tree by six-thirty. If I didn't want to be holding things up I'd better be on my way. Pulled on a second sweater, put on Uncle Jim's old leather football helmet and then tucked a folded washcloth inside each ear flap. Kept thinking I was forgetting something, but no time now. Down the steps—two at a time (but quietly). *Great!* The bundle was already on the sidewalk. No cigar smoke smell; maybe another driver this morning. Main guy probably had off on Christmas.

The bike tires were good and hard. The route should go quickly. It's quiet and clean this early in the morning and you can be optimistic. No bad motives brewing. Even the hills don't seem as steep. The light snow from two days ago was almost gone. I was pedaling my buns off without sitting down. It was gloves I forgot—not a big deal. Done that before. With nobody to disapprove I took a lot of shortcuts across lawns and private parking lots. Needed a record this morning; didn't stop to take a leak. Didn't take my usual five-minute warm-up in the Ridgewood Arms apartment building—in the lobby there was a big heating unit built into the wall, and on especially cold mornings (when no one was there to see) I would shinny up the side of it and wedge myself into the space above it for a short "thaw out." Was home at six-fifteen!

And a good thing too, because as I came up the stairs I heard Hank calling me from his room. He was ready to get this show on the road. We were either truly close or better organized than most kids, because on Christmas morning we always went downstairs together. The three of us would make a synchronized descent, restraining our excitement; especially Laura—almost a reverence in her case, holding her breath, both clutched hands up under her chin. Arriving at the living room we'd wait in the doorway, not penetrating the tree's intimate zone until Mom and Dad appeared and signaled their approval. It was a joyous and warm occasion with just the right amount of gifts. Not the overkill you see nowadays—wall to wall pieces of Styrofoam, empty boxes that had contained this year's latest "must-have" electronic devices, and a half dozen charger cords. For us, there were the not-so-enthusiastically received articles of school clothing—like the brown corduroy pants and plaid flannel shirts that I thanked my folks for, knowing they were functional necessities, but not on the top of my wish list. Along with a neat maroon plastic 45-RPM record player I received two hit records. At the moment, Patti Page was letting go with "The Tennessee Waltz." Hank got darts, which I had a hard time believing Mom approved, based on the first several tosses I saw. In fact, a few minutes later—after an urgent "look out!" that activity was being discontinued until specific firing lanes could be cordoned off.

Mom made her secret recipe pancakes. And to top it off, on this special morning we were allowed an extra piece of bacon and there were no admonitions about excess syrup. I think Hank was taking advantage of the good will—if not with the bacon, for sure with the syrup. It was a happy time. Uncle Jim called. One of Laura's friends called. Uncle Bud called again to firm up the deer hunting trip he and Dad were going on. There were non-stop Christmas carols on the radio, which caused Mom to suggest that I give up on the "Tennessee Waltz." During breakfast I had noticed Dad checking his watch and glancing my way. This time he spoke. "Roger, go get your papers."

"They're already out Dad. I did them even before Laura and Hank woke up."

He appeared surprised, even irritated. After a couple seconds he said, "Get on your bike and go get them back." And he said this more firmly than the previous instruction. Of course this didn't make any sense to me, but though I often didn't understand my father, I had learned it was best to comply first and ask questions later. I was on my way. My route had twenty-eight deliveries, which for a six-mile route was not good. Seven dollars a week if everybody paid. Ugh. *Collections!* We kids had to do them but hated it. I was only able to retrieve twenty papers. Dad would understand (if only I could).

Back home, a lot of straightening-up going on. Laura was helping Mom, as I must admit she did more willingly than did any of the girls I hung around with (though this was a small sampling I can tell you). Dad was fully dressed and giving Hank his final instructions on the designated fields of fire for his dart throwing. Carols on the radio were doing their best to sustain the mood. All the wrapping paper was picked up, minus one piece Mom had left for our new gray cat's amusement. Dad met me in the kitchen. "Okay Roger we're going back out."

Out the back door, down the steps, into the driveway, and into the same faded green Olds I've been telling you about. Dad had me point the way to start the route. After stopping in front of the first house he surprised me by getting out of the car *and starting up the walk with me.* He motioned me to get a paper and follow him. On the front steps he pressed the doorbell and stepped back, while I stood there wondering what the heck was about to transpire. The cold white wood door swung open, leaving an artificial wreath swishing on the rusted nail from last Christmas. I saw the developing seasonal smile on the face of the unwary resident falter at the sight of this unexpected pair facing him.

My dad, in his red and black plaid wool hunting jacket, big arm around my shoulders, knowing smile across his face, proudly announced that this was his son Roger, *who had been delivering their paper all year in all kinds of weather, and now wanted to take this opportunity to wish them a very Merry Christmas and a Happy New Year.* Wow! You should have seen what happened and would every time! Some better than others—but still for me, an unexpected bonanza. Before long I had a pocket full of money, including *dollar bills!*

The Saltzer's house was the last house on the route. There, Mr. Saltzer dug feverishly through his pockets without producing a bill or any change. I could see a measure of panic in his eyes, as my dad seemed to loom taller by the second. At this moment— as good fortune would have it (at least for Mr. Saltzer) the young man of the house (one of my classmates) appeared at the doorway. He was holding a brightly enameled dump truck, half out of its Christmas wrapping—a loose ribbon still draped across the hood. In desperation Mr. Saltzer shot one look at it, snatched it from his son's hands and thrust it toward me, as his last ditch, hope-for-the-best peace offering. Dad most graciously allowed it and we continued home. Dad only went to ninth grade, but I guess he just picked up a lot of practical stuff along the way.

CHAPTER EIGHT
My First and Only Summer Camp

Two weeks after school let out my parents made a surprise announcement. Not sure whose idea it was. Didn't think Dad gave much thought to how I was going to occupy myself over the summer, and if it would have been Mom's idea I would have been scheduled for more art classes. Out of the blue they informed me they had made arrangements for me to go to summer camp (although I couldn't remember ever having said anything that would have led them to believe I wanted to do something like that). But they seemed sure it would be a worthwhile experience, and anyway it was past the discussion stage. A chance to be out in the wild with kids my age; swimming in a real lake, handicrafts and nature hikes. All that stuff. Yup, *like it or not,* I was scheduled for a week at Camp Waywayanda—in the mountains. Actually, there were no mountains in New Jersey. We had to make do with a series of ridges about 40 miles west of here that somehow managed to get themselves called the Ramapo Mountains.

There was one thing that made me suspect Dad had something to do with it. He went deer hunting each year with a guy named Hubie who was the winter caretaker at Camp Waywayanda. In fact last year, Dad had gotten a big buck, so big he couldn't drag it to the camp alone. Returning to the location of the felled buck with Hubie to help him, Dad saw two guys dragging what appeared to be his deer. My dad—not being bashful, immediately accosted the two men hauling the carcass, and asked them what they thought they were doing with his deer. "Whattaya mean your deer? We shot this one ten minutes ago!" With this my dad bent over, opened the deer's mouth and pulled out his hunting license. (An act of sufficient interest to provoke a short article in *Field and Stream* magazine.)

I guess I should have been thrilled to be going to camp. For some reason I wasn't. This wasn't going to be a neighborhood thing, or a Cub Scout thing, or even a school thing. I wasn't going with Rolly or Donnie, or even anyone I knew. *I might not know a single soul there.* This was the first time that something like this had been arranged for me, and from the beginning I had misgivings about it.

I was dreading arriving and was wishing the ride was longer. All too soon we were pulling through the gate; under a big hewn log sign boasting the camp's name. Lying reluctantly on the back seat I had a really good view of it going overhead. Out of the car and to the office. The camp greeter assured my folks I would be well taken care of and that they could be on their way. No need to hang around. While I had my doubts my parents took him at his word. They were gone and I was alone with my suitcase (that we'd borrowed from a neighbor). So far in my young life I had never felt quite so abandoned.

First I received a short lecture on camp rules and given some toiletries (that Mom had already packed). Then I was turned over to another guy who escorted me to my quarters; a small log cabin with a neat front porch, and a carved wood sign above the door that said *Richard's Rangers.* There were four metal bunks inside, two with suitcases on them, but no other kids. The guy who brought me here left without giving me any instructions.

All alone and not knowing what I to do, I just stayed in the cabin and wasted two hours waiting for supper. Met our cabin counselor that night (and he wasn't named Richard). He came in, introduced himself and told a couple scary stories. He continued to show up each night to ask how our day went and make sure we complied with "lights out," but I never once saw him during daylight hours.

The recollections of my week at camp are not happy ones. I know I should have taken advantage of more activities but didn't know which ones Mom had paid for (and I didn't want to horn in on something I wasn't eligible for). Think I found out where you went to sign up for stuff, but each time I went the office was either locked, or if open no one was inside. Thanks to the guy at the Craft Shop, I did have one pastime. Using the colored plastic lanyards he gave me, I was able to spend a large part of each day, alone in the cabin, sitting on my bunk braiding necklaces and bracelets and key chains, and even one dog leash. Doing it from a bottom bunk was the best way, you could hook them in the springs under the top bunk and just braid away.

I knew there was horseback riding. Each day I would see the riders going by single file, weaving their way through camp center and towards a trail that led into the hills. I wished I could have gotten in on that. It looked like fun. The counselor who taught riding (or at least led the rides) was a handsome guy named Carl. He had long blonde hair and always wore a silky red shirt—wide open to show a big tattoo of an eagle in the middle of his chest! I fantasized about being old and looking like that. (Fat chance.) I never went riding, although after I was back home Mom told me with some disappointment, that yes indeed, she *had* paid extra for me to take part in the riding program.

Each day one cabin was assigned to clean up the mess hall after meals. I remember a couple things about the day *Richard's Rangers* got the task. The rag they gave me to wipe down the tables after breakfast must have never been cleaned. It was slimy and smelled like it had soured milk in it. One time entering the kitchen my wet hand slipped off the door frame and hit the electrified screen (to keep the bugs out). Didn't burn me or anything, but I got a scary huge jolt—like I'd never experienced before, that went all the way up through my armpit and into the right side of my jaw!

And it sure didn't get any better after lunch. I was on the porch sweeping, and lo and behold, after three days of not seeing a single soul I knew; finally— at last, *I recognized a face!* Not a real friend mind you. I'd never actually spoken to this fellow, but I'd seen him at the local hobby shop quite a few times. He was a strange bony-faced guy, with a flat sloping forehead and a too-wide and pronounced bridge of the nose. His friends called him "Horseface," and not just behind his back. I mean that's what everyone called him. He didn't mind—it was his nickname. Even the adult who ran the hobby shop called him that. Terrible as it sounded to me, that was what everyone called him. He came out onto the porch and paused for a moment right in front of me. *Someone I knew! I wasn't completely alone.* I was excited (for the first time this week) and jumped at the chance to speak to someone. With a big smile and a wave I attempted to renew our acquaintance. "Hiya Horseface."

I don't know what exactly happened, but suddenly I was seated on the porch floor trying to figure things out. Nothing hurt but my face felt numb, and there was blood. *Horseface had punched me square in the nose*—without warning, without explanation. By the time I had assembled my thoughts, he was gone. I would've explained! I didn't mean anything bad. I didn't know any other name.

Besides sitting on a bottom bunk weaving lanyards, there was one other thing I remembered from my one week at camp. I had found a piece of wood whose texture and softness suited it to carving. Its size and shape were perfect for a pistol—one of those small automatics with pearl handles that you see in ladies' purses in the old black and white movies. I just needed some neat place to work on it, *and I knew where that would be.* Not too far away, at the edge of the lake was a huge gray rock; a mammoth boulder— big as a dump truck. I ran down to it, climbed to the very top and began whittling in earnest. It was a gratifying pastime with good results. For the finishing touch I dragged the blade sideways across the wood to smooth it. It was looking good and I could already picture it after a little sanding and some varnish, on my bookshelf back home.

I wolfed down my lunch to get back to my new project as quickly as possible. I found it right where I had hid it under my pillow. Not much left to do on it. It was as fine as I could get it. And I was a little disappointed (like when you've reached the last page of a good book). I grabbed it, left the cabin, walked down to the water's edge, and crawled back up on top of the big rock. Standing, looking out over the lake with my arm extended, I aimed it and took imaginary shots at various targets on the other shore. In the midst of one volley (which I guess I was animating louder than I realized) I felt a hand come down on my shoulder. Startled, I just managed to keep my balance and avoid falling into the lake.

"Whataya got there?" I didn't know who this guy was, except he was big and belonged to the cabin next to ours. Just yesterday I had seen him pushing another fellow backwards so fast the kid's feet couldn't keep up with his body, and he went over on the seat of his pants—which humorous event likely saved him from worse damage. "Lemme see it."

He wanted to see my gun. I didn't really want to turn loose of it—especially to this guy. But I had no choice, his hand was out waiting for it. I offered it and he took it. He admired it for a moment or two, looking at the thin grooves I had painstakingly cross-checked into the grips. Then like me he aimed across the lake and fired two or three imaginary shots. What happened next was completely unexpected. As soon as he had mouthed the last shot, for no reason at all, he just cocked his arm back *and threw the gun halfway to the middle of the lake!* As you might imagine, I was never so happy to have a week come to an end, see my folks, and be back in my own neighborhood.

CHAPTER NINE
A Face in the Window

Kids generally listen really hard whenever their parents' voices go hushed, or if we see them react with unusual concern. Well I was one of those kids and Dad frequently gave me occasion to respond accordingly. He had a way of registering a look of shocked disbelief whenever some information came his way that was outside his database. As good a man as he was, it was not because he had spent his youth reading or perfecting *cause and effect* reasoning. He had his own facts; a long list of things that irrespective of their lack of statistical or scientific basis, were certainties to him. While growing up, what his "Pop" had told him, or other finger shaking adults had said, became his encyclopedia.

An example of one was his explanation for those bright vertical shafts of light created when sunshine pokes through scattered holes in an overcast sky. One time, driving along and seeing a few at a distance, he pointed them out to me and explained (almost confidentially) how this was *the sky sucking up moisture*. Even at my young age I doubted this could be the case, but his certainty and apparent satisfaction in being able to educate me, and my respect for his intent, prohibited me from displaying any misgivings. As an adult he continued to add to his database. Input would be virtually uncontestable if someone told Dad they'd *heard it from a doctor* (although I do recollect him telling Mom some gem the janitor at the plant had told him). Dad functioned based on the toils and tales of his father's generation, and therefore often found himself at a loss—struggling to make sense of a new proclamation.

The Bruces were our right-side next-door neighbors, though not exactly Dad's kind of people. They had moved in and displaced his good "old-shoe" true friends Jim and Barbara Fitzgerald, and their always smiling, chubby, freckle-faced daughter Janie. The relationship got off to a shaky start the first year. Mr. Bruce decided to asphalt his driveway, which up to this time was in appreciably the same rutted dirt state as ours. The driveways were side by side, spanning the distance between the side walls of the two houses. The contractor offered Mr. Bruce a large discount, if he could get Dad to go in on it with him—get two done at the same time. *Not to happen.* Guess Dad figured we couldn't afford it (and I could just keep leveling the ruts with cinders from the furnace). Mr. Bruce therefore had to pay the premium for one driveway and also pay for a long curb between the two driveways, to keep our sooty debris from spilling over onto his new shiny black surface. Fortunately, as awkward as it had been, Mr. Bruce didn't seem to hold a grudge. Not too long after the incident when they got a brand-new Buick with electric windows—that still had a piece of paper on one of them showing how much everything cost, Mr. Bruce sold us their blue 46 Dodge "for a song" I'd heard Dad say. 1946 was the first year after the war that they started making cars again. It was far and away the best car we'd ever had; at last replacing that ugly-fendered, oxidized, olive green 38 Olds coupe that had for so long embarrassed me.

The Bruce's had three sons. Two were adults, already out of high school, maybe even college, and just visited from time to time. When I was introduced to them they were very polite, but I sensed that meeting me was not much of an occasion for them. They wore neckties and their names were Wharton and Dexter. (Sort of gives you an idea right there why this wasn't exactly Dad's kind of family.) The Bruce's youngest son Donnie was a year younger than me; a neighborhood friend, not someone I hung out with at school. Of course in school you didn't usually hang out with kids a year behind you. Donnie was different, but an okay guy.

There was a situation within the Bruce household that I never understood (and wasn't supposed to understand) but knew was really serious. One day I overheard Mom explaining it to Dad, and it was evoking one of those looks of shock and disbelief he was capable of. It had to do with Mrs. Bruce. One offshoot was that I was not supposed to speak to her, which would have been hard to do, since she had recently stopped coming out of the house.

But I did see her almost every day. In their house there was a second-floor window at the landing at the top of the stairs. Seems just about every time I came in our driveway and got the nerve to shoot a glance up at that window, there pressed against the glass (and giving me the creeps) was Mrs. Bruce's face—staring back at me. Though our eyes appeared to meet, there was no wave, no smile, no parting of the lips. I never understood why she never came out of the house, or why she was always at that window, but I knew it was something that it was okay if I didn't understand. The only phrase I could attach to it—that I'd heard during my parents' hushed conversations, was *"change of life,"* whatever the heck that was. As best I can remember, long as they lived there, I never saw Mrs. Bruce out of the house again.

CHAPTER TEN

The Birds and the Bees in Five Minutes

I certainly wasn't dating—that was for sure. And I can't even list two girls I spoke to this week. But I *was* a little concerned about what grown-up acts would have to take place, when you would be alone with one in the dark. A little scary. Sure, I heard the older guys talking at school, and some of my friends surprised me with what they seemed to know (or lie about in a real convincing way). This was 1947 and there were no sex education classes that I ever heard of; certainly not in the sixth grade, and as best I knew none in the junior high either. I think back then parents were supposed to do it, and some questions Mom and Dad had recently been asking led me to believe they just might be working their way up to this very thing. I was afraid it was coming and that when it would, it would be a very awkward session. One night just before I drew my bath water (we didn't have a shower) I heard my folks whispering, and Mom say something along the lines of "This might be a good time Kenny."

I was in the tub soaping down when in comes Dad, cigarette in one hand, small address book-sized pamphlet in the other. *I knew what was coming.* No way to get around it. He plopped himself down on the toilet (lid down) and left me to just fiddle with the soap and fear the worst. He leafed through a tiny red book, for what seemed like a too long time. Finally, having found a good starting point and apparently gotten his thoughts together, he looked up at me and began. It was a one or two sentence preamble that I didn't see how it was going to pertain to anything about to be revealed. Satisfied with this he began reading. Word for word. Sentence by sentence. No personal commentary. Lots of male and female terms (but no human examples). He read about bees and flowers and pollen, and things that neither the pamphlet's author nor my dad saw fit to tie together. I knew all this was supposed to be part of a bigger picture, and I for one was in sore need of some specifics that would help me there.

Halfway through Dad may have recognized that he'd lost me, or he himself may have become unsure about how it was all going to come together. In any case he gave up on the pamphlet, closed it, turned on the seat to face me more squarely, and delivered about the most serious, heartfelt cautioning I had yet received—from anyone. The concern on his face was as genuine as I had ever seen, and this uncommon urgency had me "all ears." It had to do with young boys "amusing" themselves (and I think I knew what he meant here). According to Dad, this was something I had to avoid at all costs, *for God sakes!* And he knew the consequences. He had personally seen these guys as adults. *Completely crazy. Out of their heads! Just aimlessly wandering around!* Having given me this warning, it was over. He was up and he was gone. I'd been briefed, and I was worried.

CHAPTER ELEVEN
An Old Person in Your House

Later on in life I wouldn't see it so much, but when I was a kid most of my friends had someone living with them in their house. I mean someone besides their brother or sister—an *old* person! If it was a woman, she was always sitting in a rocker in the parlor, near a window; never seemed to be anywhere else. Usually with a shawl over her shoulders, legs straight out, feet crossed. Never spoke to us kids. If it was a man he would speak to us, but usually with a raised finger, cautioning us about our current activity. Those elderly men seemed to spend most their time in the garden, bent over tomato plants, or in the winter telling us kids about blizzards. They always needed a shave, and their trousers never fit right, and they always had a hard time walking—one hand on their hip, the other reaching out for some support.

Well we had one of these house guests ourselves—Grandma Deedy; a tiny, thin, bow-legged, bespectacled, gray-haired woman who lived in a front bedroom in our house. The skin on her temples was so thin you could see the veins under it. She had been with us as long as I could remember. But I can't remember the day or week or circumstances surrounding her departure (which was final). I am ashamed when I reflect on my lack of interest, an early example of me failing to recognize something of value. Even then I chose other things to be more worthy of my time and interest. I never took the time to look at her name written, so I'm not even sure if it was "Deedy." It could have been "Deady" or "Didi" or any spelling. I never asked Mom if she was part of her family or Dad's family. Based on her thin frame and sharp features, quiet manners and intuitiveness, I always assumed she was Mom's side of the family; could have been her mother's mother or her father's mother, or another relative who had outlived her own children.

The concerns of Grandma Deedy's life rarely gave her reason to leave our property, or even venture outside the house. In fact, except for traversing a short path to and from the kitchen, or short spell in the living room wingback chair, she rarely left her room. It was a tiny but well-windowed room in the front corner of our house. It contained only a few pieces of furniture and almost no belongings. I recollect a narrow single bed, a small chest of drawers, an ugly cast iron radiator and a rickety old table holding a small black sewing machine. I'm sure she had more than one dress, but if so they all looked alike—dark with lots of small flowers. Leastways that's the only pattern I remember. She never went anywhere. Never did anything. She moved about freely but while apparently "knowing her place"—making an effort never to be a bother. Never loud. Never sick. On the very few occasions when I took time out of my busy world to share a few words with Grandma Deedy, it was always my gain.

There was one thing she did have—an ornately painted tin box, the size of a cigar box but metal. A box which may have originally held spools of thread or some other sewing paraphernalia but now held Grandma Deedy's few keepsakes; things that few people knew about. Things that would not be passed on. Things that would disappear. Two of them were letters and I remember each one.

One was from her uncle, written while he was a Union soldier in Virginia during the civil war. It was on a kind of paper I had never felt, and it was written with obvious great care for its appearance. The way he shaped the letters was just beautiful. The vowels were perfectly rounded. Each consonant was sloped at the same angle, and taller than we make them now; like you'd see on a certificate or greeting card. But this was a real letter, done with a fountain pen (and maybe done on a dirt mound at night by candle). As she read me the letter I had a feeling of respect and affection for this young soldier none of us would ever know—for his vocabulary and perfect grammar, and calm sensitivity. The words were put together in a strange manner, like the writings of famous authors I would later be required to read. It was about battles and cannons full of chains being fired, and young men hurt and dying. Grandma Deedy said her uncle was only fifteen when he had written that letter and sixteen when he was killed.

The second thing Grandma Deedy had in the box—Lord knows how she came by it, was one page of an even older letter, written on brown paper and folded in quarters. It was a letter written to Thomas Jefferson by his mother when he was running for President. Like I said, none of this stuff got passed on. Never saw it in any of the boxes when we moved. I wonder who has it now. I'd love to know where that letter is today. And I'd give anything to be able to speak to Grandma Deedy again; to have her tell me about her life before our house, about her parents, and her own house, and if she remembered when she was a kid like me. I'd really listen and let her know I cared.

CHAPTER TWELVE
Learning Patience

If there was one thing in this world that I wanted—just *one* thing, it was a Daisy *Red Ryder* lever-action BB gun. I can't *tell* you how much. Donnie Bruce already had one, or at least there was no doubt he was about to get one. His dad had promised, and with no strings attached—no special list of chores to take care of first, no waiting period. His dad was going to bring one back from his next business trip to New York. (BB guns were unlawful in New Jersey, but the New York state line was just fifteen miles up the road!)

I had been campaigning for a BB gun for as long as I could remember—with no success. To help get the message through to Dad I had made up a scrapbook. *Boy,* did I make up a scrapbook! For the past six months I'd paged through every issue of *Field and Stream* and *Boy's Life,* and any other outdoor magazine I could find, cutting out all the advertisements for BB guns, and even some pellet guns (which due to their increased muzzle velocity, I knew I had no chance of getting). I ended up with over twenty pages of color advertisements and articles pointing out their safety and constructive role in a young man's upbringing. It was a "beaut;" my first sales tool. To make even more points I had memorized *The Ten Rules of Firearm Safety* and recited them sharp as could be in front of Dad and Grandpa. Although I had no idea about rule seven: *Alcohol and gunpowder don't mix.*

(Why in the heck would anyone want to take bullets apart and be mixing rubbing alcohol with gun powder?)

Finally—October. Two weeks before my twelfth birthday. The day all the world knew I was finally going to get my BB gun. Everyone had heard Dad say it a dozen times: "Not until you're twelve, that's when Pop gave me my first rifle and that's the age." I'd been listening to that phrase for over a year now, and that's a long time when you're eleven. I have to admit he never came out and said he was going to get me one on the *exact day* of my twelfth birthday. If he would have said that I would have been positive. Still I was sure that's what he meant. One thing about my dad, he wouldn't go back on his word. If he said something—even while "flying off the handle," *that was it.* He wouldn't renege. He might grumble and look sour, but he'd live with it. To make sure it wouldn't slip Dad's mind I hauled out my scrapbook every night, laid at his feet on the living room floor, and made sure he saw me tracing my finger over the pictures of the various models.

No one was more shocked than I (except perhaps Mom) when October 14th rolled around and passed, without Dad making good on what I thought was a sure thing. A wool mackinaw, a horn for my bike, a new thermos, *but no BB gun!* I was crushed. I'd waited a whole year. How could he have missed? I'd done all the "PR" a kid could do. I'd really worked at being good. The month before my birthday I'd done more fixing and cleaning (in the cellar, in the attic, in the garage) than the whole rest of the year. And a week before my birthday dad had made a mysterious trip up to Suffern, the first town across the New York State line. I would've bet anything it was to make the BB gun purchase. I think Mom had a few words with Dad in private about dropping the ball and leading a kid on. I'd lived for this day for a whole year! Talk about disappointment.

But wait. I've got one more chance—*Christmas!* I would still be twelve (even *more* twelve). This would *have* to be the occasion. The folks would know it would be the perfect Christmas gift. After some initial sulking I was now feeling confident; could hardly wait. Dad had dropped some hints, and Mom hearing them had smiled at me knowingly. If I could just wait a couple weeks *the BB gun was as good as mine!*

In our household, even with Dad and Mom both getting ready for work and we kids getting ready for school, we still ate breakfast together. Mom did a great job now that I think about it. First week of December, at one of these family breakfasts Dad told us to take a look outside. Pulling aside the window curtain I saw a true winter wonderland—half a foot already. It must have started snowing in the middle of the night. Huge wet flakes were being illuminated as they drifted downward past the neighbor's garage light. It was coming down heavily. If it didn't stop soon it would be a real bummer trying to do my paper route after school. (No more morning route, thank God. I'd graduated to an afternoon route.)

After breakfast Dad was a little rushed, packing his lunch box while still trying to get the last corner of his shirt tucked in. Yesterday he went to work with no belt and Mom really got on him for that. Everything in order he gave her a quick kiss and started towards the front door. Going through it he paused just long enough to call out, "Roger, when you get back from your paper route this afternoon, shovel the drive." *Geez! Shave my head. Send me to military school. Anything! But not the driveway!* A hundred feet of dirt, gravel and ruts, that I had been leveling with furnace ashes and was almost impossible to shovel. All the neighbors had splurged and installed asphalt drives by now, but not us. We hung in there year after year, grading our Conestoga trail.

"Okay Dad I'll remember." I hadn't forgotten about the coming holiday and my overdue birthday present. *Not going to screw up now.*

The paper route gods weren't with me; snowed all day, which never seemed to happen anymore. In class I peered out the windows not believing my eyes. When I got home the papers had not yet arrived. Remembering Dad's request I scanned the buried driveway (trying to imagine where the edges might be). Numerous undulations in the eighteen-inch-thick white blanket indicated the frozen ridges and humps, which would later send painful vibrations up my arm when the coal shovel rammed into them. Yeah that's right: Why buy one of those wide, aluminum snow shovels? "The coal shovel in the cellar will work just fine."

Hmm, a thought! A little devious perhaps, but a thought: If my papers don't come soon, I might not have enough time to take care of my unquestionable obligation of delivering them, and *also* shovel the driveway when I got back. I've *got* to do the papers first, even Dad knows that. Unfortunately, in the middle of this conjecture the paper truck arrived. Only ten minutes late. Fold em—got to fold em. Take my time. When it rained I wrapped them in plastic with an elastic band. Maybe I could do that for the snow too—that would take an extra ten minutes and cut even further into what time would be left to do the shoveling. The final good idea occurred to me while I was folding. With a lot of roads in need of plowing and none of the walks shoveled, it would be hard to pedal the bike, maybe too bad to even attempt it on the bike. *Bingo!* That's it. I'll claim I had to *walk* the route. If I can't use my bike, there's *no way* I can get back in time to shovel the driveway.

By the time I finished trudging the route it was after six o'clock. I didn't dilly dally on it, but I have to admit I didn't hustle either. Pitch black. Dad would have been home for an hour. I could see the house lights as I rounded the corner. Dad's car was parked in the street out front. (Not a good sign.) Squeezed through my special gap in the hedge, through a patch of soft light under the dining room window. Inside the back door, up the steps and through the pantry; into the friendly warmth and smell of your own home.

In the dining room the whole family was at the table. Having heard the back door, Dad was already turned towards me as I entered the dining room. His expression was not good. It was stern. He spoke: "Didn't shovel the driveway, did you?" I was silent. "No BB gun then." I was in disbelief. Stunned. I knew the permanency of Dad's proclamations. I guess I learned something here about just going along with the program, not trying to manipulate the situation, and the dire consequences that could follow. Once again Dad was as good as his word. I never got the *Red Ryder* lever-action or any other BB gun.

CHAPTER THIRTEEN
The Latest Word

Cub Scouts was one thing, but now in the Boy Scouts, we were treated a lot differently and did lots of projects on our own (without everybody's dad there). And one thing I really liked, we received special awards—visible proof of our achievements: *Merit Badges!* There were a ton of subjects you could pick from. Just study really hard, take a test, pass it and you got these neat colorfully embroidered patches for your mother to sew over your pocket. Or if you had so many they wouldn't fit on your shirts, you showed up at the meetings wearing one of those wide sashes over your shoulder—onto which your mom had transferred all the patches.

One subject everybody picked was *Life Saving.* The badge required you memorize and be able to demonstrate the five lifesaving steps. I was really good at memorizing and figured this was going to be the easiest merit badge I could get. Unfortunately, so did everybody else. At every scout meeting there was a long line of kids at the Life Saving station; each waiting his turn to kneel down by the mannequin and perform the five steps (while calling out the title of each one). This would be no problem. As far as urgency was concerned, the five-item sequence made sense to me. Two meetings in a row I was going to be the next kid to get my turn when the meeting ended. I had stood there waiting my turn, watching and listening to the same litany of five calls, over and over again:

1. "Get the victim out of harm's way."

2. "Send for help."

3. "Restore the breathing."

4. "Stop the bleeding."

5. "Treat for shock."

Tonight I was going to make it for sure. I was first in line! I waited while they got the mannequin properly situated and made up. When it was just right one of the monitors motioned me to step forward. With understandable confidence (having observed and heard the same steps countless times) I kneeled by the victim's side. Without hesitating I called out the required five steps while simultaneously taking the appropriate actions. Finished, I jumped to my feet awaiting the 'thumbs up.'

"Sorry Roger. Not right." I was dumbfounded. I *knew* I had the five steps right. I had heard them recited over and over again for months—including last week! What could they mean?

"The word just came down; the National Red Cross has reversed items two and three. But you can try again next month."

CHAPTER FOURTEEN

My Father's Father

There was a tradition in our family: Sunday afternoon dinner at Grandpa and Grandma's. The main course was always the same: roasted chicken (from his own coops), strange kinds of vegetables (Swiss chard), and good desserts (such as rhubarb pie). But the food wasn't the main thing, it was the gathering of the entire Yahnke clan. (Grandpa pronounced our name "yonk"—just one syllable, but my friends always said "yankee.") These Sunday afternoons were not only another opportunity to be spoiled by my uncles, but to see my grandpa in action. It was 1948 now, the war was over and "the boys" were back. Among them ("Thank God," I'd heard Mom and dad say) all three of Dad's brothers. For several years Grandpa had hung that small flag in the porch window; the one with three stars showing the family's personal commitment to the war.

Gramp never mentioned it and I don't think Dad gave it any thought, but Mom said Grandpa came over from Europe when he was twelve, from the Alsace Valley in France, and my dad was the first Yahnke born in the USA! Grampa arrived speaking no English, just French and German. Mom said he was so proud to be an American that he vowed he would never speak another word of those languages. Maybe a good thing too. I think in those days if you wanted to go to school you just learned English real fast. And in all the times we spent together, I never heard

Gramp say a single word in a foreign language. He never bragged about the old country; never even told me one story. I guess he was just about the most *American* person I ever knew.

Mom—who seemed to know more about Dad's family than Dad did, told me that while he was just a young man, Grandpa had started his own business in Ridgewood—a taxi business, and not in a bad location either—right at the train station. The office was under the station, built into the underpass embankment beneath the platform. The shiny black cabs were lined up right where the businessmen came down the steps. Ridgewood was a "bedroom community" (or at least that's what I'd heard adults call it) just across the George Washington Bridge from New York City. Lots of commuters returning by train needing rides home. According to Mom it was a daring venture. He started with brand new Model-T Fords. A few years ago he retired, sold the business for a goodly sum, bought some farm acreage and dabbled in a way of life his family had known in the fertile plains west of the Rhine.

Today was Sunday, quarter to one and we were on our way up to Gramp's house for the famous chicken dinner. Just fifteen minutes straight up Route 17. This was still the times when children finished (or quit) school, found jobs within the county (if not their hometown), married local girls, and settled down almost within a stone's throw of each other. Dad's three brothers lived in two neighboring towns and Grandpa in one just another ten miles north. As soon as we turned off the highway I could see the house; a very ordinary concrete block house with white wood siding. I think he could have afforded more, but Gramp wasn't much into "putting on the dog." He said he bought it because of the property: nice level ground and eight acres of good plowable soil. To my eye it slanted a lot and there were plenty of rocks in it (which he often paid me a penny a piece to chuck out). He grew lots of corn and tomatoes, plus some other vegetables, and berries! And besides the crops there were a bunch of chicken coops right behind the house. Won't talk about how Gramp killed the chickens; watched that once.

Most kids would have been upset to have the last day of their weekend taken up by a trip to the grandparents, and I'll admit, sometimes I was one of them. Especially because out of the two-day weekend, Saturdays (at least Saturday mornings) were always shot; I belonged to my dad—for him to use as he saw fit. Reported to him after breakfast and was assigned a variety of tasks such as chipping the old putty out of the window frames on the porch, cleaning the garage, creosoting the house shingles, putting more insulation in the attic, or shoveling the furnace ashes out of the cellar. Dad had always worked for his pop on Saturdays; his dad made him, and having so benefitted from it he was now carrying on this tradition for my benefit. Sunday mornings were Sunday School and church.

Even though Sunday afternoons were the only free time in the week, I always looked forward to a chance to see my three really neat uncles. They would be there with their wives or wives-to-be. All were sturdy and good-looking, had been football heroes and war heroes. I grew up with them and my father, never sleeping through the alarm on the first day of trout season or the first day of pheasant season. To my father's disappointment I eventually opted out when it came to deer hunting. After what I'd seen the first few times, it didn't look like a fair fight. Our dappled and spindly tan prey appeared delicate and vulnerable, and I was concerned as to whether or not I would be able to pull the trigger should the situation present itself.

Dad was the oldest; the only one not to finish high school. I think the one thing my grandfather might have regretted was allowing (maybe even encouraging) my dad to quit school. According to Mom, Dad didn't have a great childhood. Mom said he was born with one leg shorter than the other and wore a special brace and built-up shoe until he was nine or ten. I saw it once—in a trunk in the attic; an ugly contraption of corroded metal and dried-up black leather. Dad never pointed it out or made a single remark about it. Though I would have loved to have heard about his growing up—from *him,* he never talked about it. On those few occasions when something did provoke him to relate a tale, I was "all ears." Unfortunately these sessions were all too rare. I don't know why I just never up and asked him about when he was a kid. Mom told me his legs evened out and Dad became a very good baseball player—a pitcher, and everyone said he would have had a career there if he would have stayed in school. His next-door neighbor and one of his teammates was Johnny Vander Meer, who to this day is the only major league pitcher to throw two no-hitters in a row!

The next oldest to Dad, was Bud. His real name was Walter. No one ever told me why they called him Bud. He was the biggest of the bunch. Over six feet and acted it. (If you were even feet eleven in those days—that was big!) He was the captain of the Ridgewood Alumni football team. I remember Saturday evenings at Grandpa's old house in Midland Park. Just about dusk Bud would come clumping in out of the cool fall air, his uniform steaming, plop down in a kitchen chair and throw his legs up across another. Slumped there, his grass-stained uniform wet and smeared with mud, he'd field questions about the game.

Seemed Grandma was always concerned, checking his hands and wrists, and then over at the stove heating up something called Epsom Salts. As he shed his equipment I can remember being intimidated by the large, strange-looking hunks of black plastic clattering to the floor. As nice as Bud was to me, something about him kept me from getting as close to him as I was to Dad's other two brothers.

If Bud wasn't the smartest, he was ambitious. Spent the war in an office in Europe. Came back and joined a big insurance company in New York City. Went to college at night and took business courses. He was on his way to become a vice president of something. He was soon to marry a girl from a big (and rich) Catholic family. In years to come I would often hear Dad comment that Bud spent too much time at the country club with her family and their kind of friends.

Uncle Jim. Now there was a *real* guy! He was an All-American at Colgate. Spent most the war in the south pacific. Mailed me lots of souvenirs. On these Sunday afternoons we kids could always count on Uncle Jim to spend some time racing around on the lawn with us. He was a big hit with all the nieces and nephews and always treated me like I was special. And maybe in one way I was, though I didn't think much about it at the time: Since Dad was the first of the boys to marry and father a child, I was the first of the second generation of stateside Yahnkes. I think back then this family tree stuff was a lot more important than it is now. I cared very much about Jim and do to this day. Oh! Jim was missing the tiny finger on his left hand. One day Grandpa had sent the boys out to collect firewood. Seems my dad was about to split a piece at the same time Jim reached for it!

Jim wasn't married yet, but he was dating a tall and attractive looking brunette from the notorious Callahan family. She had dark red hair and light skin and wore bright lipstick (and had freckles you could see when her blouse was open). There was something about her that I can't explain, but when she looked at me I felt a strangeness I was not familiar with. She was there with him today, and he would later marry her. But life would not treat them well.

And finally, the youngest of the bunch—Uncle Bob. He was really hip! My favorite. The happiest and luckiest, and best-looking of the bunch. He went from high school to prep school, and was an All-American as well. Uncle Bob joined the Navy the day after Pearl Harbor. He was one of the first volunteers lined up at the Paterson recruiting office and ended up with his picture on the cover of *Life* magazine. And if you could see his smile and wavy black hair, you'd know why the photographer picked him. When his time was up in the Navy, he switched to the Army Air Corps and became a bombardier in the South Pacific; in fact, a bombardier in the 393rd bomber squadron; the most famous aircraft in this squadron being the *Enola Gay,* which dropped the atomic bomb.

Uncle Bob married an Australian tennis player. It was hard for me to believe she had left her whole family and her country to come to the states. She was a great sport, but she never played tennis again (except with Uncle Bob at the public courts). They laughed a lot. I secretly hoped I would grow up to know such good times with such a fine woman. Later they would relocate to California, take courses at Berkeley, join environmental groups, and campaign for things my dad didn't care about.

Now, down to business. I didn't appreciate it at the time, but each Sunday I would have a chance to observe why William Stuart Yahnke's four sons grew up to live such disciplined and purposeful lives. It was because of their father. Many years later in France, I would try to locate Gramp in the Yahnke family tree, but he was nowhere to be found. His brother Alphonse and his sister Camille were easily traced, but no William Stuart. The mystery was solved when it was discovered that Camille *was* grandpa! Arriving in the states Gramp soon found the name Camille was not going to work for a guy and changed it to William Stuart.

As soon as everyone had gotten themselves seated at the table Grampa spoke: "We'll say the blessing now." And he did; unrehearsed and apparently without fear of stumbling or saying anything inappropriate—a curt one minute speech to God. To me it sounded a little too business-like, but then I didn't know exactly what tone should be used. Grandpa was at the head of the long table. All four sons were on one side of the table, lined up ready to justify their week's activities. Across the table from them, their wives, wives-to-be, and we kids. Grandma was at the far end. Grampa called her "mother." She rarely said anything that did not relate to the food.

Grandpa started with his oldest son (my father). "Kenneth did you and Gay try that church out by the highway again this morning?"

"Sure did Pop, and we took Roger and Laura."

Gramp nodded approval and mumbled "...well one's as good as another." Gramp's European family had been devout Catholics, but here in the states he became a Baptist. And up till recently so were we. But the Baptist church was four miles away, so we switched to an old Dutch Reformed church only a half mile away.

Then, head up and eyes on my dad Gramp continued: "How much overtime you getting?"

"Not as much now Pop. We turned a surplus last month and there's not that much to go around now."

"Does the "supe" know you want whatever he can give you?"

"Yeah sure. He knows to come to me first."

"How long since your last raise?"

"Geez Pop. Remember? I just got another quarter last month."

"That's what I thought. Wait till the middle of next month and ask how long before they make you lead man. Tell him you're having a hard time now with three kids; that you can do that job. And if you have to Kenneth, volunteer for the night shift if it will give you the lead man position sooner. You can finagle your way back on days later."

"I'm working on that and it looks good."

"And how about that clothesline for Gay, have you had the time to hook up that arrangement she was talking about last week?"

"No. Son of a gun Pop, I forgot it till right now. Hon, why didn't you remind me?"

"She's got enough to do with Roger and Laura and now Henry. You have to remember those things son."

"And Gay, is my son treating you all right?"

"Well...."

"C'mon Hon, don't tease."

"Yes Dad, he's a real sweetheart."

"Don't forget son, she comes first before anyone or anything. Don't you forget that."

"Did you get the front end aligned on the Dodge?"

"Did it Thursday Pop. Went to that Bear place. Rides good now."

"Never want to put those things off Kenneth. A matter of safety. Think of your family."

"And how's your savings account? Still putting in twenty a week?"

"Sure am Pop, and remember I told you that Mat Orr was going to tear down that old barn on his property? Well I gave him a hand and was able to salvage two windows from it. Got five bucks a piece for em from Ed, and put that in the savings too."

"Good. I'm proud of you."

Evidently Dad had passed the review, and Grandpa moved on down the line.

"And you Walter, did you get that hound back to Al Jones."

"How did you know about that Pop?"

"Never mind. A good hunting dog is hard to come by. You're lucky he let you use it."

"I know. I returned it last night. And guess what Pop. I'm officially a Catholic now."

"You finished those courses already?"

"Yes, and Lucille and her parents are very happy."

"Well, if that's what it takes, I'm happy for you. I'm not sure if God cares which, but you're off to a good start. If it's what your wife wants it's worth it. And Walter—about work; I know you want that big position, but it seems to me you're spending a lot of time away from home. Is that going to have to continue? That's not a good way to start off a marriage."

"Well I didn't think I'd been hitting it that much on weekends Pop. Maybe. No this is just temporary. I'll have lots of time to be with Lucille, you can bet on that."

"I heard you were down to the bank last week about a loan."

"How'd you hear that Pop?"

"Don't concern yourself with that, what do you need a loan for?"

"Not really a loan Pop. It's a new thing—installment buying. I was just qualifying. I want to have a new car when Lucille and I get married."

"Well, I hear lots of people are doing it, but I believe you should just put off buying something until you can pay cash for it. That's what I've always done. Just takes a little patience. A little sacrifice and you can sleep at night."

"I think I'll be able to pay cash for it Pop. I can."

"And those golf clubs you bought from Herb, have you paid him for them yet?"

"Geez pop, I got that money to him last week."

"That's good. It's easy to let those things ride Walter. And it's not acceptable."

And so it went—a couple more questions for Bud, then on to Jim, and finally Bob. Grandpa let all his boys know he was aware of just about everything they had going on, and whatever it was, it was going to have to pass muster with him.

In later years, in my lack of regard for many things, I would remember these Sunday afternoon sessions, visualizing the short and sturdy bald man with the big nose at the head of the table, still guiding and encouraging his four grown sons. Never mind they were all in their late twenties or thirties. He had a passion for responsibility and honor, and above all—the family's good name. He was going to make sure each of his sons lived in such a way as to never discredit it. Best I could see, as long as he lived Gramp didn't relinquish his perceived duty to continue raising his sons and not feel responsible for their actions and the courses their lives were taking.

CHAPTER FIFTEEN
The Kind of Place You Can't Forget

I guess each of us has at least one place that sticks in our minds no matter how many years go by; a spot that calls up sweet memories of carefree times and innocent pleasures. A hideaway where the world's troubles were none of your business. For me it was Lake Erskine and the wonderful lazy summer days I spent there. Grand weekend adventures. I can still remember the Saturday morning excitement when I was told to get ready for the one-hour drive up to Gramp's cottage at the lake. Or better yet, sometimes—like this year, packing for a whole week! And this year might well be the last of these adventures. Dad had been hinting that next summer I would be ready to graduate from paper routes and cutting lawns to full time summer job.

At the lake I'd go for walks, go fishing, go swimming, and have the chance to watch kids I didn't know. Mostly nothing to do except think up things to do; like find a small, forked branch, skin it and fashion a sling shot for chipmunk hunting—which endeavor usually had me doing nothing more than sitting on stumps and watching them. (Never found the nerve to take a serious shot.) No schedules, no chores. Nothing a kid *had* to do up at Lake Erskine.

My father was the oldest of Gramp's four sons. All three of his younger brothers had been in the service. Mom said that because Dad worked in a defense plant he was 4F and was exempt from the draft. Now with the war over his brothers were no longer in New Guinea or Germany or those other places. They were all back here in the states, and sometimes one or two of them would pop in at Lake Erskine. And *boy* were my uncles great! Whenever asked, they would drop whatever they were doing to play badminton or volleyball with us kids. The empty lot next door had been set up with a net and a horseshoe pit. The place was made for fun. These sports activities with my uncles were always special. I dreaded hearing the call for dinner, knowing the fun would be ending.

I remember clean mornings under a warm sun, walking the rust-colored dusty roads alongside blackberry bushes. I'd take one new turn after another and feel the excitement as I allowed myself to get lost. I'd wander into unfamiliar areas of strange sights and sounds, then savor the flush as I would round a bend and recognize a familiar landmark. It was on these treks that I would have the opportunity to befriend the dogs that were always coming up to you out of nowhere. *Neat* dogs too; silver and black German Shepherds and red Irish Setters. (You wouldn't see the likes of these running loose nowadays.) But find one, be nice to it, and it would stick with you all day, almost like it was yours. If you stopped it would stop, sometimes lay down by your feet till you got going again.

As the first of a new generation, I think I was special in Grandpa's eyes. Any morning that he had fishing planned I was sure to be invited along. What a thrill, sitting on the rear seat of his old wood rowboat, rocking backwards with each strong pull of the oars; feeling adventuresome as we left civilization far behind. We'd go way out, halfway across the lake, to a spot as far as you could get from any shore. Finally, I guess satisfied with our location, Gramp would check the angle back to the club house (barely visible at this point), draw a bead on a white dock on the far shore, and then give a few more pulls on the oars to finalize our positioning. (No GPS back then.) *We'd arrived.* After two hand wipes on his baggy gray pants, he'd chuck the anchor overboard and let out just enough rope to stop us over his famous perch hole. Never saw him make them, but Gramp always had pretty good sandwiches (minus the fact he never bothered with mayonnaise or mustard) and a big thermos of iced tea. If the fishing was good we'd stay till past noon. And what a fuss Mom and Grandma would make when we finally tromped up the back steps, wanting to see how many fish we had, and asking whether we got any perch, or were they all blue gills again.

And the evenings at Lake Erskine held their share of adventure as well. As often as I could, after supper when the grownups were still in the kitchen, I would slip into the living room, delay a few minutes just in case, then slip out onto the porch. If no one called, I'd sneak down the steps and run down to the lake. Far as I could tell, all the kids were strangers here and I was one of them. It was a new experience. There on the clubhouse porch in the dark, I could move around without anyone seeing me or questioning my presence. I watched excitedly as the teenagers teased and cavorted inside (jealous of the boys lucky enough to be in the midst of all those giggling girls). I particularly envied one good looking guy with shiny black pants and a silver belt. Boy, would I have liked to someday dress like that. One time I got brave enough to slip inside, and when I did I was almost able to imagine that I was part of the group. I stood right near the door and just watched—still in the shadows and a safe distance away. I could never speak to them of course, or even let myself get noticed. I was just a kid. Later, when I saw a group of girls begin ringing some sort of centered activity, I somehow got the nerve to sneak up and stand right close behind them (which gave me a strange warmish feeling inside).

One daring evening fling in the shadows had a minor downside; got a bad splinter off the railing on the clubhouse porch. The next day I made the mistake of showing it to Dad. He marched me straight back to the kitchen. I knew what was coming and I was scared. The cottage didn't have a regular kitchen table, just a wooden booth with two benches. Dad motioned for me to sit on one side and then plopped himself down across from me. He didn't wait. No briefing. No reassuring words. He just yanked my arm across the table, pinned it down with his forearm, and then using the biggest needle I'd ever seen, he set about digging out the gray wood sliver in my palm. And he didn't fool around. No tiny picks around the edge. He went straight in for it!

Mom said Gramp had discovered Lake Erskine when they were still cutting the road in and he had bought the first lot ever sold. I don't know exactly when that was, but based on the weathered shingles, sag of the porch and slope of the roof line, I'm sure it was a long time before I came along. If it would've been more recent, I would've remembered seeing Dad packing off with his carpentry tools to help his father. Since Gramp had blazed the trail in and erected one of the first dwellings, he considered himself one of the founding fathers of the community. He had bought and built before the crowds; before any ideas about a clubhouse or a boat dock; before any of the streets had names; and especially before the darned *Association* was formed. Of course my dad had been properly indoctrinated, believing as well that the family's seniority and contribution to Lake Erskine was well known and revered by all the residents. Each year there were a bunch of pesky new regulations, but Gramp said these were mainly for the summer renters from the city.

I must admit, in the midst of non-stop great days and evenings, there *was* one unsettling occurrence. One afternoon Dad decided to take Laura and me to the lake. The Association had just spent a lot of money trucking in real seashore sand for the swimming area and we were going to take a look. Besides what I will relate in a minute, let me tell you about Dad's bathing suit. I know that sometimes we still call them "trunks," but have you ever heard them called *tights?* Well that's what my dad called his bathing suit. "Hon, where are my tights?" They were an ugly maroon and made out of thick itchy wool (that didn't dry for days). No elastic either. Got stretched out of shape immediately and stayed that way from then on. The leg holes were loose and from the right angle I could see some of my dad's private parts. And the bathing suit had a *belt!* A too-long white web belt that dangled down on Dad's bare thigh. If I thought when I grew up I would have to wear a suit like that, I wouldn't even go swimming. As it was, I was just glad no one knew us up here.

Laura was only a tyke and Dad was carrying her on his shoulders, one of his big hands clutching both her ankles, the other (embarrassingly) periodically on my back, guiding me along. It was only a couple hundred yards from the cottage to the picnic area at the high end of the lake. We arrived, turned in through the gate and were on our way down the gentle slope towards the clubhouse. From there we would take a planked walkway along one side of the lake to the swimming area. The walk from the gate down to the clubhouse was a cozy one under a thick canopy. We wove our way between the redwood tables, scanning the ground ahead to avoid tripping on the gnarled roots half-hidden beneath the pine needles.

I felt Dad's hand now on my chest, holding me back. I looked up to see why. We had been confronted by two adult bathers leaving the area. One of them was not a likable sort. Viewing him and listening I felt suddenly uneasy. He was standing right in front of Dad in what looked like a threatening way, pointing at him and making stern comments. It was not hard to learn his complaint. He was accusing Dad of not being a member! I was pretty sure we were members, and I think I heard Gramp saying he had just picked up our new badges the other day. More than that, the stranger was telling dad that *he could just turn around and march right back out that gate with his two kids.* I don't think I'd ever heard anyone talking to my dad like that. (Or even imagined that it could be done.) My father didn't answer, just pointed down to the large orange metal badge carelessly pinned (almost sideways) to the side of his bathing suit. The mean guy just scoffed and informed my dad that *that* was *last* year's badge—not any good, and anyone could have picked one of them up out of the trash.

I sensed my dad's patience being tested (and I'd seen him lose his temper once or twice before). It got worse. The man was now poking Dad in the chest, not just once but repeatedly, as his tone became more belligerent. About five seconds of this and I felt Dad's palm leave my chest. I looked up in time to see his arm snap back and a fist shoot out—contacting the man right smack on the chin! It was like the guy's legs just vanished and suddenly he was sitting in the pine needles looking up at my dad with one of the most perplexed expressions I had ever seen. Dad's left hand had never let go of Laura's ankles. I felt my hand being taken and we were on our way again. With what I knew about my dad I would not have made the same mistake as the stranger. I had long ago decided that my father was not someone you threatened.

I don't think I had a moment's ease till we left the lake. Even back at the cottage and especially during supper, I kept thinking I heard cars slowing down in front of the cottage. I was still waiting for the police or some authorities, or a group of Association members to come knocking on our door. Nothing ever happened. Minus this, Lake Erskine continued to be the same sunny, easy, and fun place for us it had always been.

CHAPTER SIXTEEN

Working at An All Girls Camp

Mom was real smart. We all knew that. For the last six months she had been working as the personal assistant for some rich lady up in Montclair. We didn't know much about Mrs. Frey except she ran a big company in New York and owned a camp in the Pocono Mountains. A few days ago she had asked Mom if she would like to spend the summer as her Camp Administrator. When Mom told us about it I could see she was excited. She always liked new challenges. Although Dad wasn't too hot on the idea—it would mean he'd be without Mom for the whole summer and saddled with us kids. They talked it over and Monday morning Mom told Mrs. Frey she would do it, *if she could take her three kids along with her.*

Mrs. Frey bought it! Hank and Laura and I would be going on a ready-made summer vacation; or at least Hank and Laura would be. I was older and yup, you guessed it, I'd be *working* at the camp—full time. Dad had Mom ask Mrs. Frey if there might be some yet unassigned tasks a young and willing worker could accomplish. She allowed there were and thus I was going to be on the payroll (although not very much on it I can tell you). And this wasn't just any camp, this was a *girls'* camp. A one hundred percent all girls' camp! I'd finished junior high, would be a freshman and turn fifteen in three more months. This summer job was going to be a real change. No more just doubling up on the paper routes or stocking shelves in the stores, this was going to be a real adventure.

We made the trip to Camp Teedy Usk Ung in our new—well almost new—46' Dodge. Dad could only stay overnight. He had to leave Sunday afternoon. I could tell he was going to miss Mom and still wasn't too keen on the whole idea. Mom didn't seem as upset about the coming separation as I thought she should. She was still excited, flitting around the premises, familiarizing herself with the facilities and learning what her duties would be.

The camp was situated on rising land above a lake; one side of the property then being a curving hundred yards of tangled shoreline. Camp center was a well-manicured area of freshly cut grass, dissected by sand walkways bordered with white bricks. The admin building, dining hall, and craft shop (in whose storeroom I would sleep) were situated at the lower edge of this large centerpiece slope. Below them a tree shaded path led down to the boat docks and swimming area. On the high side of the grass area was an arcing row of cabins in which the girls would sleep. *Only fifty yards from where I would be sleeping!* Behind these cabins was a foreboding thicket.

The camp offered lots of activities. I saw red clay tennis courts, rifle ranges, archery ranges, and badminton and volleyball courts. But the big deal at Teedy Usk Ung was the riding academy. At the edge of camp center was the start of a winding dirt road that penetrated the ring of dense woods and ended a hundred yards later—in a large clearing. In it and surrounded by a freshly painted white fence, was a first-class riding arena (with red and white obstacles and water pits and shrubs). To the left were the stables and hay barn, and to the right, the bleachers and judge's stand. Mom said rich people sent their daughters here to perfect their riding skills. And *boy,* was I to find out there were some "horse-crazy" girls here. I heard that some of them would sneak out of their cabins at night and sleep in the stables with their horses. (I chanced a looksee a couple nights without finding any such girls.) And when their camp stay was over you should have seen all the crying and sobbing. Mom told me that many of these same girls went on to ride and win blue ribbons in the big horse shows in Madison Square Garden.

I was disappointed on one score. I had just assumed I would be the only male on the premises, or at least the only eligible one (and as such was already imagining how popular I might be). But no such luck. Right off the bat I was introduced to Norman. He was about thirty and good-looking, and six-foot five if he was an inch; didn't seem fair. Norman was a basketball coach for a small college in Kentucky. Here at Teedy Usk Ung he was the head counselor, taught swimming and other sports activities. So now, not only did I have another male to compete with, he was big and good-looking, and a little mysterious. There was something strange about him—in fact plain weird. Mom said he was a conscientious objector during the war; refused to carry a gun and ended up driving an ambulance in India. While there he had been converted to something by some guy named Gandhi (whoever he was). Norman professed some religion I never heard of. If there was something he didn't like, or didn't want to do, he always said that *he dreaded it like the plague.* I could imagine (and later see) how all the girls would want to be hanging around Norman.

And it almost got worse. The second day I was introduced to another guy, Harry. And Harry was exactly my age, so I couldn't fudge on any comparisons. I was to find out Harry was a lot like my friend Wesley, in that he seemed to know or have done more than a guy our age should have. I got the idea that Harry didn't have a mother or father (or at least living in this area). He had grown up in the nearby town, raised by different townsfolk. Helping my odds with the girls was the fact that Harry wasn't very good looking. He had a bad complexion, bad teeth, and smoked!

There were just two other guys. Mr. Hale and Buddy. Mr. Hale was in charge of the riding academy and Buddy was his sidekick. (Harry was the stable boy.) I didn't see them much. They lived off the campgrounds in a trailer about a mile away. Mr. Hale was older and married, but Buddy was a pistol. He was about twenty-five, always telling dirty jokes and making sexual comments. Buddy was only a little bigger than me, but real strong, especially in his left arm. His right arm was malformed and only about a foot long. In spite of this I still viewed him as my chief competition. He had a neat drawl, and always kidded with me, but somehow I didn't completely trust Buddy.

Finally I met Fred, and the moment I saw him I knew I was in trouble. Fred was a large, hunch-backed old man, the year-round caretaker for the property. In the winter months when the camp was closed he lived here all alone. Now, during the summer he lived in a shack a couple miles down the road to Hawley. Fred had bowed legs and when he walked he rocked from side to side like an ape. One or two of his front teeth were missing (top and bottom), and he only had one eye, or at least one of his eyes was always closed. Never once saw him smile. He had a permanent scowl and stared menacingly, even at strangers. You could just tell life had been hard on him and he bore it a vengeance. He wore the same outfit every day; a blue short-sleeved work shirt and baggy gray pants that hung on wide suspenders. Don't know why, but I was sure Fred didn't approve of the likes of me. (Guys like Harry were okay.) I didn't feel safe in his presence and went to some trouble to avoid crossing paths with him.

I was anxious to know what my job assignments would be and was surprised to find out that just about every job I could think of would turn out to be my job. The hardest of them would be taking care of the tennis courts, dragging a 200-pound concrete roller back and forth every couple days. Besides that I'd cut the grass (*miles* of grass); collect all the garbage and trash, haul it a half mile back in the woods and burn it, and clean the admin building. Before meals I'd work in the kitchen for Malcolm, the colored cook whose oft repeated bit of advice I remember well: "Roger, there's, there's a, there's a time and, and, and, and a place for everything." (Malcolm stuttered.) During the meals—all three of them, I'd wait on Mrs. Frey's table where Norman and all the other counselors sat. After the meals, I'd be back in the kitchen doing the dishes. After they were finished I'd sweep the entire dining hall and porch.

A Bad Start with Norman

The camp was going to open in two days and I was assigned to Norman (with whom I was finding little in common). We were supposed to get the swimming area ready, which would include towing out the raft. Norman had told me to wear my bathing suit. It was June, but it was only seven-thirty in the morning, and up here in Pennsylvania the morning air was a might cool. I was afraid to guess how cold the water would be. I followed three or four steps behind Norman down the path to the lakefront. When we got down there I was confronted by a dying body of water, being overtaken with reeds and algae and lily pads. The shoreline to either side was a swampy area of mangrove-like brush and rotting tree trunks. (Could visualize snakes sliding through it.) I wished I had put on some sneaks; not anxious to have my feet in contact with this type mire.

We'd start by towing the raft out, anchoring it, and installing the ladder on it. The raft, which had been beached for the winter, was a ten-foot square white wood platform with four 55-gallon drums mounted underside. We drug an aluminum rowboat to a spot just a few feet offshore from it. In so doing my fears were confirmed; the water was like ice. Norman helped me a little bit (but not much) in attaching a rope from the stern of the small boat to the raft. Mostly he gave directions from a dry point up on the beach (as I leaned into the raft with all my 119 pounds). As big as the raft was, I expected he would assume the job of rowing. I was wrong. He gestured for me to sit by the oarlocks and then plopped all 200-plus pounds of himself on the rear seat. This pitched the bow a good foot out of the water and had I not grabbed the gunwales, could have launched me up and out. I assumed the rowing duty with nary a word (not daring to verbalize my opinion we'd gotten our seating assignments backwards).

I was expecting Norman to give some guidance as to where I should steer, but no instructions. He just sat there in one of his trances. I started towards a spot that was about as far out as one could expect the girls to swim and then lined up with where the lifeguard stand was lying on its side. Though I was afraid there would be no way of avoiding it, I was dreading the thought of getting in the cold water. To further discourage me, in addition to the temperature problem, on the way out I saw a couple wakes near us, as if some type of reptile was moving along just under the surface.

"Right about here. This will do it." (A little proud of myself. I'd picked the right spot.)

Norman pulled the boat up against the raft and clambered aboard it, momentarily half submerging one side of it. Still on his knees he toppled an oddly formed concrete anchor over the side. *Kaloosh!* A short tug down on that corner, a bob back up, and we'd secured the raft. He motioned me to join him on the raft. We sat there together—the two of us; a giant and his small helper in the middle of a dying lake. Silence reigned. I wasn't going to volunteer anything if he wasn't. I had already noticed that from time-to-time Norman would just stop whatever he was doing and slip into some sort of reverie—sometimes right in the middle of a sentence. A couple minutes of silence and then he'd pick up where he left off. I just waited. The sun was just high enough to clear the treetops (but not doing much to warm the air). An eerie two-foot-thick layer of mist covered the entire surface of the lake.

Through the spaces between the boards I could see the water just beneath. It was not inviting. A cloudy green liquid that all too quickly swallowed up the shafts of light, allowing them to penetrate only a foot or two. *Whoa, what's that!* A fish or something big made a loud splash just behind us. I whipped my head around but too late. Norman didn't budge. I examined the stainless-steel ladder lying on the raft between us, and the plastic sack of hardware we'd use to secure it to the side of the raft. Norman awoke, grabbed the ladder, worked it over to the edge of the raft, slid it into the water and braced it against the side of the raft.

"Here, hold it like this. Right here." I did, squatting and holding the ladder so it would not slip into the lake. Norman ceremoniously began untying a valuable-looking leather pouch. Once opened and spread out—each corner carefully flattened, he began to unfold the oily brown paper inside it, to finally expose the contents: a set of gleaming nickel wrenches. He sifted through the shiny tools, finally selecting one. He held it up without speaking, just admiring it. He then extended it toward me until the wrench occupied a spot three inches in front of my face. "Use this but guard it with your life." The words were softly spoken but a solemn warning. To me this meant two not-good things: First, I was the one going in the water to attach the ladder, and second, I was going to use that wrench, and I'd damn well better not drop it. "I'll hand you the bolts when you get in the water. After you have them in, I'll hand the nuts down through the spaces between the boards."

What? *Down through the spaces in the boards?* I wasn't just going to have to get in the water, I was going to have to go *under* the raft, which would mean ducking my head underwater! Norman took the ladder. Staring down into the murky surface my imagination ran wild. I lingered on the edge before lowering my feet into it. A chill went all the way up to the back of my neck. Instant goose pimples. I thought I could make out the tops of seaweed wafting back and forth just a few feet below the surface. I was not eager to lower my body into those environs, but I had no choice.

I was in, one hand hanging onto the edge of the raft, the other one clutching the nickel-plated wrench from Poland. Both legs were curled up as high as possible; didn't want my feet to be any lower than necessary. I didn't know if it was five or fifteen feet deep (and didn't want to find out). Now I'm treading water (and trying to do it with my legs still coiled up). I put the wrench in my teeth. Took the four bolts and got them through the holes in the ladder and the boards which formed the side of the raft. Only in the water three minutes and my whole body was shaking.

"Okay get under over here. Cup your hand. I'll drop you the nuts and washers down between the boards. And don't miss em!"

It was now or never. Under the raft! I took a gulp of air and did it. Lowered my head, but not my feet. It was particularly scary under the raft. The off season had left the undersides of the boards with molded mud nests, beetle carcasses, and webs with dead spiders. *And* then *I thought I felt my foot hit something in the water!* Wham, both my feet up against my backside.

"Here they come. Going to give you one set at a time." I cupped my hand as high as I could up under the space between the boards. (Still treading water.) The nuts and washers plopped into it. Got em! Uh-Oh, just noticed the two lower bolts were beneath the surface. I'll do those last. Get the two top ones first. I went to work, tightening the nut by hand as far as I could. Would only need the wrench for the last couple turns. Very carefully slid it over the nut. Slow measured turns. There it is—top two done. I was cold, shaking, and imagining all sorts of sea life (like carnivorous turtles and electric eels) circling just below my feet. But I was half done.

The two remaining bolts were only a foot under water and I could see them clear enough. I'd tighten the nuts by hand again—as much as possible. Harder than I thought. The ends of these lower bolts were rusty and the nuts didn't go on as easily as the top two. I would have to use the wrench just to begin these; did it a half-turn at a time. Handle of the wrench locked in my fist. Finally got it. *Only one more.* Norman dropped the last nut and washer through. Caught them. Threaded the nut on. Tightened it by hand as far as I could. This one was not going on easy either. Backed it off. Tried again. It jammed again. Try as I may, it was not going any further by hand. Gotta use the wrench just to start this one too. *Careful!*

Even using the wrench I was having a hard time turning the nut. Each half turn took all the strength my thin wrist could develop, Five, six turns—making progress! Still hard to turn. Last turn. Pushing with all my might. Suddenly the resistance quit and the nut (and wrench) spun freely—away from me. The extent of force I had been exerting caused my hand to slide right off the end of the wrench! It was free! *And off the nut!* I was paralyzed (and a real bad time to be paralyzed). For a second the wrench seemed to suspend itself there, a half-foot under water, not moving. Unfortunately, neither was I.

Another split second and it had come to life, recognizing its debt to gravity. It sliced downward. I took a swipe at it and missed. It flipped and glinted as a shaft of light hit it. It was two feet down. A second inadequate swipe, as I mistakenly tried to keep my face out of the water. Missed it again! No two ways about it, *I had to go under.* I could still see a fading glint, but it was on its way. *This would be my last chance!* In a second I was under, eyes open, moving lower. Another reach for it, but not as deep as it should have been (not wanting my hands any lower in the murk than necessary). But because of this reluctance *I missed it a third time!* No choice now but to go down—caution to the wind. Even if I drive my fingers into the worst type of muck, I've got to do it. It was getting dark. Could barely see it. On the bottom. Fingers in the mud, entwining slick grass. Out of air. Can't see anything. Lungs on fire. Gotta come up.

Even before I hit the surface I could hear Norman yelling. He must have guessed what happened. I knew if when my hand had first slipped off, if I would have just put my face under—right *then*, I could have gotten it. Or even having missed it on the first swipe, if I would have dove then—right then without waiting, I could have gotten it. I was too late making the commitment. It was horrible. Norman didn't chew me out, just stood there stunned, hurt and sulking. Finally into the boat and letting me row him to shore. He didn't say a word to me on the way in, the rest of the day, or that week.

A Night Out with the Guys

On the weekends Mr. Hale and Buddy (never Norman) went to some backwoods bar; a log cabin-like, draft beer and juke box place not too far from camp. I'd heard them joking about it, giving each other an elbow and talking in hushed tones. In any case—right now, Buddy was asking me, *Me? Did I want to go with them Saturday night.* Why me? Never saw a party that needed me. I was shocked that they even considered including me. While still trying to decide if he was serious, Buddy leaned close and whispered to me with a wink, that *there were always a lot of good-looking girls there. (*A good way to get my attention.) Would I find the courage to say I'd join them? I couldn't believe my ears as I heard myself telling him "Yeah, sure I can." I knew Mom mustn't find out, but how would she? She didn't hang around with the likes of Buddy.

Spent all day Saturday a bundle of nerves; a little anxious but also a little scared. At 8 P.M. I slipped away from camp center and up to the highway to wait for Mr. Hale and Buddy, and Harry. (He was invited too.) Waited. Nothing. I was about to slink back into camp when over the hill came the black

Pontiac. The door swung open, I was in and we were on our way. Five minutes and some awkward joking later we turned off the highway onto a narrow country road. A few minutes on it and Mr. Hale began slowing down—found what he was looking for and made a turn onto a one-car-wide dirt lane with dense woods on both sides. The headlight beams illuminated no more than a hundred feet of ruts and the low hanging branches. It ended abruptly, forcing us into a small tree-stumped clearing that boasted just one poorly lit building; a log structure with a front porch that I guessed correctly was our destination for the evening's forecast good times. I was a little disappointed. The Bear's Lair didn't look like a place that any girls I'd be wanting to meet (or any girls, period) would be hanging out. Our arrival brought the number of parked cars up to a grand total of three. We all piled out, joking and back slapping—to me, a forced attempt to bolster each other's anticipation of a forthcoming good time.

I was last up the steps and across an unlit warped board porch. Our entry was delayed a minute or two while Buddy bounced up and down on a creaking old couch. Inside I concluded there must've been only two people in each car, because there weren't even half a dozen people inside. *And none of them girls!* I trailed behind, not sure if we were going to walk right up to the bar and order three fingers of Red Eye, or what. Mr. Hale took over which was good. He was older (and at this point in the evening I still trusted married adults). He strode over to a round table and whipped out a chair. The other three of us circled the table and did the same. I was concerned about what I was going to order when that time came. *No way I was going to get away with ordering a coke.*

There *was* a juke box, but no one had put any money in and the silence was doing nothing to enhance our surroundings. Evidently it was having the same effect on the others since Buddy got up and went over to it. After hollering a couple smart remarks over his shoulder, he made his selections and took a stroll to the men's room. There were no waitresses at the Bear's Lair, so Mr. Hale set about taking the orders. I knew it was now or never. In a manner I didn't recognize, I replied, "Any kind, as long as it's cold." I was a little proud of my quick thinking. What's more, Harry seemed to approve of this and said, "The same goes for me." (Maybe the first time in my life I initiated a course of action.)

Buddy came back. The music was playing. The tray of beers arrived. Everything was in place. *This was it.* Mr. Hale made a toast to some old friends. Buddy laughed and said "down the hatch." I tried to take at least two swallows before putting the glass down. It frothed up in my mouth and was strange on the way down. I had heard it was natural not to like beer right off (and from this experience I now agreed). The way the other guys were chugging them down, my glass would only be half empty when they finished theirs. I considered lowering the glass below the table and tipping it so some would drain out onto the floor.

A second mug appeared in front of me even though my first one wasn't finished. At first Mr. Hale and Buddy were joking and apparently having a fun evening (or trying to have a fun evening) reminiscing about old times. Then somehow the conversation turned serious, and it didn't seem to me like they were having a good time. Lots of complaining. Oh No! A *third* round. I'd finished my first beer and was making my best attempt at the second one when it arrived. This was an entirely new experience. Up to this point I had only sampled a single mouthful from a rowdy friend of Dad's. I felt like I might be making some kind of important transition, but into what and if I even should, I wasn't sure.

I finished the second glass about the same time I realized I had to pee (as Buddy would say "like a racehorse"). I eyed the door Buddy had gone through to the men's room, slid back my chair, stood up, *and got the surprise of my young life!* Almost fell straight back over the chair. Somehow, thankfully, I caught myself and was able to avoid a horrible embarrassment. There was noise in my ears and I was light on my feet, as if there was a cable from the ceiling suspending me just above the floor. I glanced down at the others. *Had they seen? Were they watching me?* It got worse. I scanned their faces, I could see lips moving and expressions changing, but I couldn't understand any words; in fact I may not even have been hearing any words! The room suddenly tilted, and I pressed both palms on the tabletop to steady myself. I recognized the symptoms: *I was drunk!* In the thirty minutes I had been sitting there—without me noticing it, the alcohol had been doing its job.

Hands off the table. Upright now. Committed to it. Starting across the floor. Working hard at basic navigation. *Big* job just staying centered midway between the row of bar stools on the left, and the dance floor on the right. Every step was calculated. I was shifting my weight and corralling inertia to form a trajectory that would end up hitting the bull's eye on the far wall (the men's room door). Though I couldn't risk looking back, I guessed by now they were all staring at me (probably taking bets on whether or not I'd make it). Almost lost my balance completely on one adjustment. Could feel their eyes on my back. *Thank God I hadn't fallen.* Made it! At the urinal it was a longer mission than

I'd had for some time. Being more skilled after my first trip, I did a better job on the trip back to the table.

In my present condition I was an inept outsider, unable to add anything to the conversation, or try as I may—even follow it. I felt excluded but could understand why. *May take a while to get in the swing of these Saturday nights out,* although so far it wasn't all that much fun, and I wasn't sure I'd try it again. Things that were happening at the table and alongside us on the dance floor were beyond my ability to follow. I remembered the scenes in the old cowboy films when the hero was told to take a swig of whiskey just before they cut out the bullet, and I could now easily understand how effective that would be. Don't know how long after that we stayed; could have been fifteen minutes or an hour. I suddenly realized the other guys were standing up, and concluded we were leaving.

Outside and standing in the middle of the dark weedy field, I began to feel ill. Took a couple full breaths of the cold air, which didn't help. We must've stayed late because there was only one other car still in the lot. Buddy was wrestling with me (and it took me a while to even recognize it)! I was no match, even for a one-armed guy. I think Mr. Hale was reprimanding him. Out of the corner of my eye I saw Harry pointing at me and laughing. Next thing I know, Buddy is hoisting me up on the front fender. He held me there a moment, and before I could figure out what the plan was, *the car was moving!* I grabbed onto a chrome molding to steady myself. Where'd Buddy go? In the car? How did he get there? They *all* were in the car! Of all things, Mr. Hale himself (the one person I considered a real adult) was at the wheel, and laughing like mad. The car yanked to the right and he must've floored it. Grass and dust were flying in the headlight beams. We snarled around the field in a tight circle. The way the car was turning, I was afraid to jump off even if I could have done it. (Was just sober enough to know I could easily end up under the wheels.) I slipped and slid onto the center of the hood. I now had a grip on the hood ornament like a rodeo rider clenching the saddle horn, waiting and praying for this stupid prank to be over.

Oh No. We're not stopping, we're *leaving!* We're on our way out the dirt road. The car bounced and lurched in the ruts. I was over on my back now. Something sharp was cutting my side. Next thing I knew we were turning onto the main road. The engine roared and I could feel us accelerating. I was hanging on to very little, but hanging on to it for dear life! I was barely staying aboard. The hood was heating up fast. The rushing sound in my ears was now the wind and my vision was distorted by tears. The night was flying by. Mr. Hale (who I had by now lost all respect for) hit the brakes and I was half down in front of the grill. Sole of my shoe was on the bumper. Struggled to keep my foot from slipping off behind it (in which case it could continue down to the speeding pavement just inches below). I closed my eyes and squeezed and prayed harder.

The camp—camp center. Thank God! I rolled off the fender and down onto the grass. We were back. I'd made it. Buddy and Harry were laughing and slapping their legs. I was never so happy to be lying on the ground. I'd made it. I never would find out if I had just passed initiation or if this was the kind of things older guys did when they went out drinking. You might guess, the rest of the summer and for sure—Saturday nights, I pretty much stayed on the campgrounds.

A Close Call with Fred

I did venture off the campgrounds one more time; don't know why. (Wish I hadn't now!) One afternoon I agreed to accompany Harry into town—his town; the nearby small village of Hawley, which like the camp lake was barely hanging onto life. Shouldn't be too dangerous—still daylight (and without Buddy). I could buy some stuff I needed and finally get to meet some of the friends Harry was always talking about (who it turned out, all had bad teeth, smoked, drank beer and whose cars were temporarily not running). Still, in his own right Harry must have had something going for him. Almost everyone we passed gave him a wave and had some comments to pass on. He was known by young and old alike and got enthusiastic greetings from old guys sitting on rickety chairs in front of rundown storefronts. I could see there was a wide assortment of people who had occasion to know Harry, but they weren't the kind of people who waved at me back in Ridgewood (or even the kind of people in Ridgewood).

Harry wanted to show me the billiards place where he got beer "no problem." He walked in like he owned the place. I followed, sampling a heavy, damp, old-fashioned odor. The walls were crowded with faded photos, deer antlers, and shelves with stuffed birds. The furniture looked a hundred years old. The wood floors were dry and dusty and scarred; only a few remnants of varnish along the baseboards and in the corners. Harry had something to say to each guy we passed, and every one of them acknowledged him with a couple fingers to the brow or a slap to his backside. We plopped ourselves down (like we did it every day).

Several fellows were having a boisterous time not too far from our table. The center of attraction was one young guy about eighteen, in a red plaid hunting cap with those ear flaps hanging down. He saw Harry and gave a big wave. Harry waved back and whispered to me, "That's Lloyd—Fred's son. He's leaving tomorrow." It was 1951, the Korean conflict was growing and the draft was picking up. Boys were leaving from both big and little towns, going really far away to fight in some "police action," to stop the "domino effect," or something like that. This was Lloyd's last day before shipping out. A few minutes later he managed to navigate his way over to our table. As my dad would have said, he was *three sheets to the wind.* He began talking Harry's ear off, about the good old times I think. I don't know how Harry made any logic of it. Lloyd was missing words (and even a couple teeth like his dad) and his sentences just weren't making any sense. Not being Harry and Lloyd in the condition he was, I couldn't decipher any of it. Lots of back-slapping (and I think once, almost some crying). I felt uncomfortable. It was the first time I had been this close to a conversation with a real drunk. I tried to pay polite attention. For me it couldn't have been over soon enough.

Back at camp that evening while we were doing the dishes, someone asked us about our trip to town. Harry said we had seen Lloyd, rolled his eyes back in his head and smiled knowingly at me. I one-upped Harry, tilting my head from side to side and acting like I was drunk, *not realizing Fred the caretaker (Lloyd's father) was standing in the doorway, watching my charade.* It was the first time in my life I'd seen that much hate, and directed right at me! I knew immediately I had used poor judgment. I don't think I meant to ridicule his son. And going off to war is probably a pretty good reason to get drunk. I was scared and wanted to get to a safe place as soon as possible. I raced through the last few chores and ran up to the admin building, where I spent an hour with mom. She was more than pleased (and a little suspicious) to have me suddenly choosing to make this extended visit.

After lunch Sunday I helped with the dishes and then swept the dining hall (and huge screened-in porch as well). By the time I finished and returned to the kitchen everyone had left except Malcolm. He was on his way out and asked me to go down into the cellar and bring up a sack of sugar. I liked Malcolm and said "Sure." The dining hall's stone foundation served as the cellar walls; a large cold and dark space used for storing foodstuffs. There were three long rows of pallets, stacked almost to the ceiling with cartons and sacks. The original stone walls were crude and cracked, and the timbers holding up the ground floor were split and rotted. It was like a cave. If you listened hard you could hear water dripping. The floor was hard-packed dirt. It was poorly lit by a few bare light bulbs dangling from a single electric cord that ran the length of the cellar. I considered it an act of bravery just to go down there. Especially alone. I never felt safe.

I reached the bottom of the steps and started down the row leading to the sugar. As usual I had left the door at the top of the stairs open. (Any extra light you could get was always welcomed.) While trying to separate the flour bags from the sugar bags, that shaft of light was squeezed out and I heard the door shut. I had a premonition and my heart froze. A second later the dangling lights went out. I was standing there in quasi dark. The meager amount of light filtering through the dirty ground level windows barely silhouetted the tops of the stacked cartons. I was scared.

"Now I've got you. And I've got you where you belong, with all the other rats in the cellar. I'm going to get you now."

It was Fred! I was petrified. My heart was in my throat. This was it. The little acting I had done last night—mimicking his son must have been the last straw. The loudest thing in the cellar was my heart pounding in my ears. It was so loud I had to strain to fix the location of the shuffling noises Fred was making as he worked his way down the aisle. "I've got my rifle here, but I don't need it."

Hearing him speak gave away his position. I backed up carefully making sure not to topple anything, turning around at the far end of the second row. I could hear the sound of cellophane wrappers and debris crunching under his feet. He couldn't have locked the door from this side. If I could just get to it I'd be okay. But the stairway was on the other side of Fred.

"This place was all right before your mother and you came here. She and her bookkeeping and new regulations, and you— you city kid. I know what has to be done."

Fred was now in the third row, halfway down, not twenty feet from me. Didn't know how I could get past him to the stairs. *Oh God.*

"I think as much of you as the other rats in the cellar."

My mind was racing. I was crouched down low. I could hear him approaching the end of the row. I had to go further down the row, *further away from the stairs.* But I had no choice; he'd see me if I didn't. I was on my way. I wasn't crying out loud, but I felt tears in my eyes. I cursed myself for my thoughtless panning of Lloyd. I knew I'd learned an important lesson in life. It was just whether or not I was going to live to use it. I heard a low throaty laugh—a not-good sounding laugh. I made it around the far end of the third row. I don't think he knew where I was. I was as still as a statue. I didn't move and I didn't hear him move. Every few minutes I heard another low, mean-sounding chuckle. *He was going to wait me out.* I knew I had to do something but didn't know what. I was too scared to think well. I was now on my knees at the far end of the cellar, completely away from the door. Just waiting to be discovered.

What's that? I heard the door open and a shaft of light shot into the cellar. "Roger, where are you! Get up here with that sugar." *It was Malcolm! He hadn't left. Thank God!* I could hear him starting down the steps. *Thank you God!* I bolted up the row, knowing I would be passing within five feet of Fred on the other side. But I was at top speed and had Malcolm there as a witness. I bounded up the steps and past Malcolm. Didn't have the sugar. Didn't say why not. Out the door! Heard Malcolm exclaiming something about "...damned kids, who, who, who can understand em."

I spent the rest of the day about three feet from Mom. I didn't tell her what happened, but I'm sure she knew something was wrong. I didn't sleep well that night. I was much too worried. Every move I made the rest of the summer was based on my best estimate of Fred's whereabouts.

CHAPTER SEVENTEEN
A Real Summer Job

Yesterday was the last day of school. For most kids it would mean neat vacations with their parents, one fun day after the other at Graydon pool or whiling away the hours in the soda fountains on Main Street. Or best of all (my dream)—playing baseball in a summer league; on a real team, with uniforms, on manicured diamonds, and having your parents there watching you! But not for me, I'd be working. And even if I wasn't, I probably wouldn't be having that much fun; end up spending half my time sitting on the curb with Wes or in the backyard doing nothing with Rolly.

What *would* be my ideal pastime? Something I could only fantasize about (and did just about every day): first—*not* work, and then be popular enough to spend the summer days cavorting with those cool rich kids from the Heights. Boy, did I envy that group. The guys were always laughing and having good times, wearing pastel Bermuda shorts and mahogany colored penny loafers, *without socks*. No matter what stores Mom took me into, I never saw the clothes those guys wore. And the *girls* from the Heights were all pretty; couldn't miss them sashaying through the halls dressed in their white blouses and plaid skirts, arms crossed in front enfolding their books and hiding their emerging bust lines. And now in bathing suits, well, I couldn't imagine being there that close the whole day.

As much as I would have given to be a part of that group, I never got close. I wasn't special in any way; not tall, not good-looking, and not a football hero. Not even a football participant. Never even had a reason to strike up a conversation, except when I was assigned to some class project with one of them. And when it happened, to my great surprise they treated me almost like an equal. I was on a float committee with Barbara Gordon and then on a March of Dimes drive with Bill Graham. They were two of the most popular kids in the class (and not stuck up either). But these were the exceptions. There was a difference and I understood it. My dad didn't work with most of the other fathers. He didn't take the train to Manhattan in the mornings, and I certainly never saw him with a briefcase. Dad worked in an aircraft plant in the nearby town of Woodridge. Originally he'd been a machinist but had recently been promoted to an Industrial Relations Supervisor (whatever that was). Based on the congratulations from my uncles and grandparents, you would have thought it was the most elevated position anyone in our family ever had.

But if I was going to have to work this summer—which I surely would, I was ready for something new. Mom wasn't working for that rich lady anymore so there'd be no girls' camp this year, and enough paper routes, cutting lawns, and odd jobs. I would be in the tenth-grade next year and I was ready for more prestigious work; *hard work* that deserved some respect. That is, as long as I was going to have to work. Not sure I ever considered I could just skip it, Dad was always saying I'd have to learn the meaning of a buck. And Mom—though I'm not sure she shared Dad's conviction, mentioned it could be the start of an important savings account.

Wesley Riley, who was knowledgeable about these things said I should check out the celery farms in Paramus. He said they mostly hired foreign people but would hire American kids even if they weren't sixteen. And they didn't care about Social Security cards. He made it sound exciting although I suspected Mom and Dad would need extra convincing. No one from our neighborhood (even the adults) ever had a reason to cross Route 17 and venture into the taboo area known as the "truck farms." Still, if I was going to do something different this summer, this would fill the bill. Work hard, bent over, get my back nice and tan, carry a lunch bag, and hang around with older guys who smoked and had tattoos. I decided to check it out this weekend.

Saturday morning—seven o'clock, still cool and fresh. I was excited as I began the four-mile bike ride to the mysterious truck farms. Not sure what I would find there but hoped it would be the way I was visualizing it. Pedaled east on Lincoln Avenue then turned south on Route 17, past the famous Paramus Roller Rink—a place that for some reason my parents were not too keen on. The high school girls who smoked and had older boyfriends with drivers' licenses went there. Ten more minutes on a gravel shoulder with tractor trailers roaring by only three feet away and finally, there it was—the turn off that led to the celery farms. It was the first time I'd ever been here without Wes or Skip. I ventured in past shanties selling hub caps, old furniture and strange vegetables, whose vendors looked up suspiciously as I went by. Half scared, half invigorated, I pedaled faster. The wind felt good.

I could see it now—the farm Wes told me to check out. A table-flat half mile by half mile bright, wet verdant patch cut out of the woods. I arrived and coasted to a stop alongside what appeared to be the only path (not even a road) that led into the farm, and surveyed the area for a moment before starting in. Acres and acres of green shoots coming up out of black water, but only a couple small shacks and a half dozen workers. Two or three flatbed trucks with big tires were sloshing across the paddies. Weird contraptions of bent metal were lying on the ground and propped up against dead trees. None of the workers I saw—all shirtless and wearing baggy black leggings, appeared to be in charge. I didn't feel confident. No one looked over my way as I laid my bike on its side and contemplated my next action. I had never tackled anything exactly like this before. Somehow I must have gotten the courage, because next thing I knew I was tromping my way in. The nearest group was composed of three tall, bare-chested men. Steered towards the only one who appeared to have noticed my arrival. Stopped in front of him and surprised myself by speaking up. "I'm here to see about a job for the summer, if you have one, if I could work here."

His expression didn't change; spent most his time brushing away a fly. He motioned me towards another big guy sitting on the back of a six-wheeled half-truck, half-tractor thing. It looked like some sort of motorized loading platform, maybe custom-made for a unique job here on the farm. I started towards the thing. Ninety percent of the ground was under water. You had to walk on narrow, raised dirt paths that framed the large wet rectangles. With each step I would sink and stick a little. My right shoe got pulled off. Shoved it back on quick before anyone could notice. By the time I got to the truck, both shoes and trouser cuffs were covered with black gook. I pretended not to care. It wouldn't look good to be overly concerned with one's appearance. None of the other guys— all older men, even *had* shoes on their huge gnarled feet.

I explained the purpose of my visit again. The huge man with no shirt, dirt streaks all over his chest and face beaded with sweat, wiped something out of his eye and looked down at me in an annoyed manner. I was sure he was aggravated that I was even there. He answered painfully with a waving-away motion of his big hand. "No, no, you much problems. No here." Right now, this reception could have been enough to turn away an average applicant. And in truth I was becoming less and less keen on the whole idea myself. It was a cinch I wasn't wanted and it was a long way from home, and it was hot and there were a lot of insects. And I had held up my end of the bargain. I'd put forth the effort and tried. And maybe this summer would be the one I'd not work; get to be on a team and somehow get in with that group from the Heights. *Naw that's just dreaming.* No way Dad would hear of that. He's expecting I'll work full time this summer.

I put on a real disappointed look when he waved me away (though I was aware of a mounting feeling of relief at this rejection). I looked back up at him getting ready to make one last case for my employment (though I wasn't sure what that would be), when another hulking guy grabbed his shoulder. I waited patiently while they hashed something out in subdued tones (although it didn't have to be subdued since only one word in ten was English). A few seconds later and to my great surprise, *I was hired!* But not much of a ceremony; was told to show up at seven Monday morning, that I'd get thirty minutes for lunch and finish at three-thirty. Earn four dollars a day. That was it. I'd been hired. They turned back to their work and I was alone. I should have felt better. I had accomplished exactly what I set out to do. But I didn't have a good feeling—not at all. And any hopes for this summer were out the window.

The weekend went fast. Unlike my state of mind, my friends seemed to be in good spirits with no complaints. But then there were no demands on their time. Donnie Bruce wouldn't have to work at all, that was for sure, and Rolly would just help his dad in the evenings, assembling a real church organ (whose metal pipes started in their cellar and went all the way to the attic). Victor Longo would just keep doing yard work in the neighborhood (friendly surroundings). Wes on the other hand, worked full time at the Sears and Roebuck Automotive Center, and was therefore qualified to be my confidant. We did consider some other plans, but I think we wasted most of Saturday. Sunday afternoon we rode our bikes back and forth past Graydon Pool, hoping for the chance to see someone we might know. No such luck. Noticeably missing were the kids from the Heights. They didn't get too excited about anything, much less a public pool opening. Our town had gone all out on this pool; a huge, man-made pond, 500 feet across, surrounded by rolling soft green lawns and loads of willow trees with graceful branches hanging down to the ground. Hit the rack early on Sunday night, knowing I had a six o'clock get-up in the morning.

I was awake before the alarm went off. A quick cereal breakfast and out of the house and on the road by six-fifteen. Early in the morning the day is still what you're planning it will be, not what it might end up. (The bike ride would turn out to be the best part of the day.) I had packed two peanut butter and jelly sandwiches and an apple. Mom made me take the apple. I was pretty sure I would just end up bringing it home again. At the farm at six forty-five. Fifteen minutes early. While I was hoping this early arrival would distinguish me, it was another thirty minutes before my presence drew any attention. When it did,

I was told what my job would be. I was going to be a "planter." The perfect job to get that tanned back I was talking about. From 7:30 till 11:00 I walked—better plodded along, in mud up to my calves and water up to my knees, bent over ninety degrees at the waist, behind one of those Rube Goldberg vehicles I had seen earlier. I had a mud-caked burlap sack, at least three feet long, slung over my shoulder, dragging behind in the water. It was full of celery seedlings. Were it not for the fact it was half floating, it would have been really hard to pull along. My job as I sloshed forward was to first use this pointed metal tool to jam a hole in the ground every few inches, then reach back, take a celery seedling out of the sack and jam it into the hole.

On the back of the truck were two of the biggest and strangest appearing guys I had ever seen; looked like circus giants (not accustomed to humor). They weren't old, but they were completely bald. They had big heads, thick lips, and wore no shirt or shoes, just those baggy black pants. They spoke no English and as I said, did not look friendly—even to one another. (Reminded me of the guys in the old syndicated Sunday cartoon, *Terry and the Pirates*.) About every fifteen minutes I snuck a "straighten-up" just to see if my back could do it. Eleven o'clock couldn't have rolled around too soon.

There was one other young guy working on the farm. He was a little older—about sixteen I'd say, and he wasn't American. I was surprised when he came over and joined me for lunch. He didn't have a paper bag; he carried his lunch in his pocket—*loose*. He had a lot of unkempt brown hair and bad teeth. He spoke with an accent and didn't have good grammar. He was kind of good-looking in a strange foreigner way, and he was *friendly*. We ate in the shade of an abandoned metal shed. There was a raised bank of dirt along one side which gave us a dry place to sit. After fifteen minutes I wasn't sure I would be able to get back up. I was exhausted. My back was broken. The apple was delicious. I wolfed it down (and thanked my mom).

Gustav knew a lot about this kind of work. He'd had lots of jobs. He told me he never went to high school; didn't even start it. (In light of this his grammar wasn't all that bad.) He said this was a bum place to work and everybody knew it, and he was going to get out of here as soon as he could. Lunch was over and we went back to doing the same thing we'd done all morning. I was almost crying by three-thirty. I had never been so glad to see three-thirty in all my life! There were tears in my eyes as I sped homeward. My neighborhood never looked so friendly. My house never smelled so good. I was just waiting to spill my guts about this new job, but no one was home yet. Finally at dinner Dad did ask me about my job and *boy* did I tell him. I made it sound even worse than it was. He didn't look impressed. I think Mom was concerned. I was already thinking of laying the groundwork for the day when I might have to tell Dad I was going to quit. I could not imagine enduring this for two and a half months. No one could.

The week went the same; every day, every minute, every six inches. Up to our ankles in mud and up to our knees in water, using that strange steel-pointed tool they gave us to reach down through the water, poke a hole in the mud, then shove one of those green stalks into it. Sometimes I'd accidentally dunk my face in the water when reaching down to pack the mud up tight around them. Reach back for another seedling and do it again. My fingers were worn from the burlap and the mud, and the skin was getting funny from being underwater so much. Not that it was any longer a priority, but I sure was getting my tanned back. Not sure how long I would last.

I ate lunch with Gustav every day. It was the reprieve that got me through the day—resting up against that shed in the shade. Gustav told me what country he had come from, and that his grandfather and grandmother were still there, but I can't remember how to pronounce it. Here in the States he had a life I could barely imagine. He didn't live with his family. In fact he didn't live with *any* family. He lived with some other young workers he knew. He didn't know where his mother was; she may not even have come to the United States. His father was working just like he was, twenty miles away, at another truck farm near Tenafly.

One week! *Made it through.* Friday afternoon and payday! I almost cried for joy when I got the money: $19.60—in cash! They took out 40 cents for something. I was going to enjoy *this* weekend I can tell you. Spent just about all day Saturday with Wes and did I tell him about his darned truck farm. In the morning we helped his dad who was doing a valve job on their Chrysler. In the afternoon we went to the hobby shop and then walked up the street to the Warner Brothers theater to read the *Coming Attractions* posters. And of course we pedaled by Graydon Pool; this time seeing lots of classmates, all apparently having the best of times. After supper we sat on the curb in front of my house, closed our eyes and listened to the cars as they passed. The goal was to guess what make they were just by the sound. Wes actually could do it—almost every time! I have no idea how. They all sounded exactly the same to me. Wes left and I went in. Listened to the "Inner Sanctum" on the radio; a scary program which always began with the sound of a squeaking door opening (and was only listened to when there were others in the house). Then went to bed.

Wide awake at seven but stayed in my room till almost eight; mostly because I think they expected me to (and it would further validate my level of exhaustion). My folks allowed that working every weekday I could skip Sunday School, although they did ask me to attend the eleven o'clock church service with them. Sunday afternoon I joined the rest of the family for our new weekend pastime; a jaunt to "the property." Recently Dad had used all his savings to buy twelve acres in Upper Saddle River. Each weekend we spent at least one full day up at the property. I'm not sure how much Mom enjoyed these woodsy outings; tagging alongside Dad while he chopped trees, pulled stumps, burned brush, cut roads, widened creeks, sunk wells, and spoke of his plans to build a cabin. But as best I can remember she was there by his side on every visit. I was there behind a wheelbarrow. Too bad my dad didn't hang onto this property; about thirty years later the adjacent property was purchased by President Richard Nixon.

The Monday morning alarm was a rude reminder of my personally picked punishment. The pleasant leisure of the weekend was still fresh in my mind. The thought of all those kids lounging around Graydon Pool, just wasting time with nothing to do, haunted me. Why couldn't I—just *one* year, spend a summer like that? I remembered the cheerleaders at first laughing and flirting with the guys, then up and running, being pursued by blonde crew-cut football players snapping towels and tossing pails of water. And here I was on my bike, not being thought of or missed by anyone, winding my way even further from the good life.

The second week dragged by but I made it; wanted to quit but wasn't sure how. I guess there's a lot of truth in how you can get used to just about anything. I was numb now; just "doing time." The hours came and went. I didn't hear people talking, didn't see things happening. And then finally I would be on my bike, homeward bound, pedaling like crazy, tears welling in my eyes. Speeding past the shallow and dirty *Duck Pond* across from Terwilliger's Ice Cream, I saw two kids at the edge of the water, joking and lazily skipping stones out over the water. Evidently nothing they had to do; were probably there all day.

The third week would see a change. I was called aside by the guy that Gustav and I called "Big Oop" (from the *Terry and the Pirates* cartoon). He was six-foot five if he was an inch. Bald as a billiard ball. Never wore a shirt, never wore shoes—just big, baggy black pants. Hardly spoke at all. Just after lunch he motioned me away from my planting job (which if it would only be for five minutes, would be a cherished respite). He told me in so many barely translatable words, I was going to be promoted. Not in pay but by being assigned a choice job on the farm. I was going to work in the shade, cool and upright—no longer bent over ninety degrees. I followed him to a three-sided shed constructed of warped 2x4 posts; wired together with sandbags piled at their base, and doing their best to hold up a battered corrugated metal roof. Inside were two large galvanized tanks about ten feet long, six feet wide, and four feet high, filled with dark (oily-looking) water. One of the tanks was against an outside wall, below a large opening.

Big Oop crudely explained: The trucks would back up and dump the loads of freshly picked celery, right through the hole in the wall and into that first tank. The second tank was right next to it, but further inside the shed. *The choice job:* Get into the first tank. Take one of the hard-bristled wooden brushes floating on the slimy surface and be ready to scrub the incoming celery—every stalk, stalk by stalk. Get as much gook off them as you could and then toss them into the second tank. I would learn another job would be to avoid being drowned by the incoming celery. Even with my limited work experience I wasn't sure that this was any choice job.

After lunch I started. Into the tank. No shoes or shirt, just wearing my trousers. Got a hold of one of the brushes, which was difficult to grip due to an accumulation of celery oil on the wood. The bottom of the tank was covered with slim and small objects about which I wasn't sure, and some were moving. *Sneaks back on fast!* It wasn't long before I heard a vehicle approaching the shed. Pulled myself up to see over the lower ledge of the opening and saw a dump truck backing towards the opening. I retreated and waited. Another minute or so, some gears grinding, and *in comes the celery!* Don't know how much celery I thought I'd be dealing with, but the amount of celery that came through the opening had me fighting to stay on my feet and keep my head above water. What a pummeling I took. I was never so glad to see anything stop. There was barely room in the tank for me. There must have been a thousand stalks come in. Even if I hadn't gone under twice, the deluge had my face and hair soaked and dripping, and I had something in my eye—stinging like mad. But I was ready to go to work.

Grab, scrub, shake it under water, chuck it. Grab, scrub, rinse, chuck it. Could have done it even quicker except I have a failing of perhaps being too conscientious—too concerned that someone might discover an imperfection in something I had done. I went at the job furiously, resolved to get every speck of mud off every stalk, and determined to get my tank cleaned out, before—God help me—another load arrived. After an hour my knuckles on the brush-hand were really aching. I couldn't tell if my hand was open or shut. My fingers on the celery hand began to sting. When I checked them I could see they were becoming raw; would have to be more careful with those bristles. The *celery,* not my fingers! Thank God for small favors. A second load never arrived. I had the tank empty five minutes before quitting time. Big Oop came by and looked surprised. I don't think he was expecting to see the tank empty, but he didn't say anything. He examined some stalks out of tank number two. Even though there was no "good job," he seemed pleased and took a couple stalks away with him.

I did this job all day Thursday and Friday, while thinking about begging off because of a rash I was starting to get all over my body. Gustav saw it and said it was "celery itch"—*all the scrubbers get it.* He said at the big farms the scrubbers wore rubber suits. Finished the week and got my pay. $19.60. You're probably saying, "That was a long time ago, nineteen bucks would buy a lot." I'm here to tell you it didn't go very far.

The weekend couldn't have been more cherished if I was on furlough from the state prison. Dad didn't make me work with him Saturday morning and I made points by volunteering to accompany him to the property the whole afternoon. Sunday I got a reprieve that I sorely needed (which I suspected Mom had decreed). I was able to do whatever I wanted. That turned out to be mostly just hanging around with Rolly. (Wes was working.) Didn't spend much time on my bike, missed dropping by the new YMCA or cruising by Graydon Pool. Maybe for the best; didn't get to see any of those rich Heights guys cavorting with the girls. Observing it would have just made me wish even more that I could be there. Sunday night taking a bath I had a chance to see and feel how bad the rash had become. I could hardly stand lukewarm water. My crotch and the inside of my legs were one big red blotch. And there were small pimples on the undersides of my arms; had to hold them away from my sides. I put on half a can of talcum powder and set up a table fan to blow on my legs in bed. I was worried about getting back in the tank on Monday.

Maybe God *is* watching. First thing upon arriving at the farm, Big Oop gets me aside and indicates I'm being reassigned. Now I'm going to be a "puller." Didn't know if it was because I hadn't cleaned the celery fast enough or because I was doing it *too* fast. The Puerto Ricans sort of had a little union on the farm and had been giving me real dirty looks and complaining about something to the bosses. They put *two* of them into the tank afterwards.

Now I'm out of the mud and out of the tanks, riding on a truck (of sorts) on the other side of the farm. But while I had the dirt and water part beat, I wasn't exactly *riding* on a truck. I was into a contortionist's job. I was lying on my stomach, half off the rear edge of a flatbed, with the back of my legs wedged under an anchor bar (rusted pipe) that kept me from slipping off altogether. I was supposed to hang off the back of the truck as it moved along the rows, yanking the celery out of the ground and tossing it behind me up onto the truck. This was good for that tanned back I wanted but also let me know what my spinal erector muscles were.

There was more than one downside to this new job; something that made me very uncomfortable. It appeared that Big Oop— now riding on the truck with me, and the guy driving the truck, hated each other. They were always arguing, and I mean arguing bad! Even as a kid I could tell it was serious, seeing them snarling under their breath. I was staying out from between them, that was for sure. I worked as hard as I could and didn't say anything. But they both looked really mad all the time. I made a point of not making any eye contact.

A few days later I was to get an unanticipated release from my summer job. I was on the back of the truck, hanging upside down, clawing the water and snatching stalks, when Big Oop and the driver begin arguing loudly. The truck jerked to a halt, which was bad. You weren't supposed to stop in this area, the vehicle could bog down, and then the driver would be in big trouble. I took advantage of this delay to unhook my legs from the anchor bar and readjust my position. In fact I raised myself up to where I could see what was going on. The driver was out of his seat and clambering over it onto the platform where we were. He was moving fast and swearing in some language. In his hand he had one of those worn-smooth, pointed metal tools that I had used to make the pilot-holes for the seedlings. Before anyone could do anything he was onto Big Oop, and had driven the tool into him! Oop let out a scream and then a terrible noise as he went down on his knees, then over on his side. It was over in three seconds. For sure I had never seen anything like this! Oop tried to get up, but the driver put his foot against him and pushed him off the truck—headfirst into the mud. I had no idea what to do. Didn't move.

The driver jumped down off the truck, dropped the tool and just started walking away—like nothing happened, like it was quitting time. I was standing alone on the flatbed. Big Oop was gurgling in the water alongside the truck. A nearby worker had heard the noise and was running our way. The driver kept walking—just normal. Gustav shouted to me that we had to get out of there. More people yelling. I was off the truck and splashing through the water with Gustav. We ran out of the paddies, past the sheds and to the front of the farm where we had left our bikes. A mile later, winded and safe on the shoulder of Route 17 Gustav said he was quitting for sure. He said he'd seen this kind of thing before and cautioned me, "You won't never get on with another farm if you get tied into this." He said he was leaving for now, but that he was *damn sure coming back to get his two and a half days' pay.*

I said "Me too!" But I knew I had no intention of ever setting foot on this farm again (or even on this side of Route 17).

Twenty minutes at full speed and I was turning into our neighborhood. The driveway was empty. But *good luck!* I spied our 46 Dodge at the end of the street, just about to go around the corner. *Oh no.* The family was leaving. I might be able to catch them. Dad was on vacation this week and they *were on their way up to the property!* I could just make out Laura and Hank's heads through the back window. It was about a mile to the highway. In that long of a stretch maybe one of them will look back and see me. Sometimes there was a few minute delay on the ramp as the cars waited to get out onto the highway. *Please God, make this one of those days.*

I was pedaling that Schwinn like never before. Standing. Leaning forward. Around the corner now. Bike rocking left to right. *Pump!* But even as fast as I was going I wasn't gaining on them. My only chance was they'd be delayed getting onto the highway. *Luck was with me!* They were and I caught them. I had tears in my eyes but I was with my own family. Mom had tears in her eyes. Dad told me to pedal back to the house. He'd come back and get me.

CHAPTER EIGHTEEN
A Spring Formal to Remember

When Mom said it was a *girl,* I thought she was kidding. Sure I was sixteen now, but that wasn't getting me any phone calls from girls. But it *was* a girl, and a nice girl—Arlene Bradley. Her dad was a lawyer. She wasn't beautiful, but she was okay and smart, and everyone liked her. I often saw the popular kids—football players and cheerleaders talking to her, although usually asking her about homework or tests. But why would she be calling me? She hardly knew me. Oh we had spoken. She was polite enough for that. She would say something to me if we were squeezing through a door together, but we never walked together or anything like that. Of course I never walked with *any* girls. Although I'd often fantasize and wonder what it would be like—walking down the hall holding hands with one of those pretty, bright-eyed girls, especially if it was one from the Heights!

What? I felt my ears redden and my heart skipped a beat. *Would I go with her to the Spring Formal?* I knew about it alright. It was put on by the Junior Class girls every year, and held at the exclusive Ridgewood Country Club. You had to at least be in the tenth grade to go. I don't think I'd ever felt so flattered; numbed and not realizing there could be an alternative answer I said *Yes I would.* In fact saying *No* never entered my mind. It certainly didn't seem proper to say no to a girl who had selected you and then got the courage to call you up and ask you. Actually this wasn't my first time being asked to a "girl-ask-boy" dance. My first experience occurred in eighth grade when the Junior High had decided to experiment with such an event. I was similarly flattered when Lucy Ann Clayton had made the same call as Arlene. Somewhat apologizing for the intrusion and in outlining her reasoning she had said words to the effect of, "...*and you were about the only decent one left.*" Prior to later reflection I took that as a compliment.

A couple months ago Mom had mentioned it might be a good idea to think about taking some dance lessons. And I finally agreed, but they were only being given after school and I was stocking shelves in the Co-op. *Sure would've come in handy now.* And something even more scary, this dance was a *Formal.* While I wasn't exactly sure what that meant, from the way all the girls had been talking about it, it must have been something really special. Mom clued me in: *It meant I was going to have to wear a tuxedo.* Not only did I not have one, renting one certainly wasn't in our budget. Mom and I were worried till Dad (of all people) came up with a possible solution. "Herb is just your size, and I know he's got one. He wore it to that thing the Masons had. I'll talk to him at work. Betcha he'll lend it to us."

Wow. That would be neat. Except it was hard for me to imagine any adult being as small as I was. *How could I fit in any grownup's clothes?* Dad asked when it would be. I told him the twelfth of May; two weeks. Dad said not to worry. He'd get Herb's and bring it home for me to try on. I was at a loss to explain why—on this *one* occasion Dad had decided to get involved in something I was doing. This was a first. And lo and behold, Herb must have been small, because when Dad brought the tux home, *it fit me perfectly!* Hardly recognized the figure in the mirror. I felt a new excitement to be wearing a grown man's clothing.

When the day of the dance came around I was more than a little nervous. By five o'clock my stomach was churning. Mom had done her best to get me ready. She had held school on the corsage thing—how to hand it over and pin it on, and gave me a cram course on the Foxtrot. I think I mastered the basic steps, but it seemed to me it would be boring if all I did was left, right, left, side-together; those same steps over and over again. And finally I got some tips on being *debonair* (or something like that). I was sure there was going to be a lot of stuff I wouldn't know, but I'd had all the last-minute tips I could handle. I was as ready as I was ever going to be.

Neither of us were old enough to drive and her parents volunteered to take care of the transportation. Arlene would be here any minute. And sure enough, seven o'clock on the button I heard a car in our driveway. I checked myself one last time in the hallway mirror, and truthfully I had never seen myself looking so good. I couldn't help admiring the tailored jacket and shiny lapels. I grabbed the corsage. The Bradley family was on the way up the steps.

When Arlene spied me she took a breath—almost appeared startled. And she looked good too, though I would have hated to be surrounded by the material in her dress! It stuck out everywhere, had ruffles all around, and made a loud swishing noise when she walked. Mom was great—handled the introductions, even helped me pin on the corsage. I was proud of my folks. It was the first time I'd ever seen them talking to any adults that lived even near the Heights, much less socialites like Mr. and Mrs. Bradley. And in our own house! The photos and small talk finished we were on our way. I was proud of myself—thought I was acting pretty well composed, although Arlene seemed nervous.

It was dark when we arrived at the Ridgewood Country Club. Mr. Bradley joined the line of cars that were easing ahead, pausing, and then spilling out their young couples to traipse up the marble steps. I'd never been in such a setting. Waiting our turn I scanned the colorful entrance. Brightly lettered banners and paper lanterns were stretched across the porch and between the pillars. There had been a special committee for that and evidently they had gone all out. It was easy to see this was going to be a festive occasion. Before we got out of the car Arlene firmed up a time for her folks to retrieve us. They wished us a good time and were off. Her mom and dad had been real nice to me. We were out and on our way to the main entrance.

I felt good and must've looked sharp in this grownup's tuxedo; would have been easy to imagine I was the center of attention— that people were noticing me. It was a new experience all right, and I must say I was liking it. For once I think I knew why those rich kids from the Heights always seemed to be in such a good mood. Just inside the door there was a reception line, where Arlene told me it was the girl's job to present her escort to the sponsors. I was feeling even more special; proud to be deserving of her introductions.

By the time we got to the ballroom it was already quite full. The band was warming up. People were milling about. Even before we mingled, still at the edge of the room, I felt as if all eyes were upon me. *And it was then it struck me!* There was a roar in my ears and I felt the color drain from my face. I searched— frantically, my eyes probing the crowd, but not one—not one other guy in the whole place, was wearing a *black* tuxedo! It was a *Spring* formal! *White* jackets! *Now* I understood Arlene's surprise upon first seeing me in the house, and why I had felt as if "all eyes were upon me." I wanted to die, to disappear. But there was no way out, I had to make the best of it. I had two tough hours ahead of me. So did Arlene. She was a real trooper. An hour into it—peering across a mass of bodies, I was elated to finally spy another guy in black on the far side of the hall. It took a little pushing, but I forced our dance pattern across the hall towards him. Closing in on him practicing something cute to say. I saw he was a cop!

CHAPTER NINETEEN
Rules for Buying a Car

1952. I'd sure been waiting for *this* year! Only three more months and I'd be the magic age in New Jersey: Seventeen! *Old enough to drive.* And the good news was—surprisingly, Dad had given me the okay to start looking at used cars. Checking the "Autos for Sale" section in the classified, Mom and I'd found a "guaranteed like-new" 40' Mercury coupe, and we were on our way to check it out!

Pulling into the driveway, *uh-oh*—no such car graced the premises. Maybe they've already sold it. Mom said "Oh well we'll ask anyway." She pressed the doorbell and a few seconds later the door swung open. *In luck!* The woman said they still had it but appeared skeptical looking at me. There was no back yard, but right behind the house was an old shed with broken siding and dirty cob-webbed windows. The high doors were padlocked closed. The lady pulled out a key and began working it back and forth with no success. Oh no, don't tell me we're not going to get in. Then in front of my eyes, a click and it was unlocked. She put her weight into one big pull and the door creaked open enough to squeeze through. We were on the verge of unveiling its treasure. I hustled in behind the adults, and there it was—my own black beauty. It looked brand new! Sleek and gleaming. Bright chrome grill. I'd found the very best on our first try!

Thankfully Mom took the lead and asked the lady what I guessed were the right questions. Not involved I examined the interior through the open driver's side window. Even got the courage to open the door. Seats were a grayish-brown felt material. Hard to tell in the limited light, but nothing looked worn. The interior even *smelled* new (or at least it had some kind of neat smell). Perhaps due to the confines of the garage, the car seemed larger than I was expecting—even intimidating; looked like something it might take a while to learn how to maneuver. *But it was love at first sight.* Shiny black bulbous fenders and a gracefully sloping trunk (which Wes Riley once referred to as a "torpedo" rear end, whatever that meant). My heart was pounding. The lady told Mom she could crank the engine. I slid out and Mom got in. It started right up with a powerful roaring sound. *Hard to believe this car was about to be mine.*

During the ride home Mom gave me advice about driving and caring for a car. She agreed it was a "beaut." I had saved up three hundred dollars, and it was only two hundred seventy-five! *It was as good as mine.* I was already imagining having Rolly and Wes over, walking around it in the driveway, and especially sitting in it together at night. All that was left was to clear it with Dad.

Well I knew my Dad lived by certain rules. I'd pretty much learned the things that made him tick. But I was going to learn one more, and it would mean that while I was probably going to get a car, it wasn't going to be *this* one. Yup, according to Dad, it was good we'd started looking—nothing wrong with that. And it sounded like a good deal. But no matter what, when you're looking for a car; no matter all the good and right things, *you never buy the first car you look at.*

CHAPTER TWENTY

Didn't Want to DO It
in the First Place

Not walking this morning! No bicycle and no school bus neither. I'm riding with Wes in his car, *and there are no adults in it.* Wes had turned seventeen yesterday and we were christening that event. Wes's dad had let him buy his car during the summer. For three long months now it had been parked alongside his garage. And you can bet we spent every spare minute we could admiring it, doting on it, and trying to *supe* it up. Got the heads milled, put on "duals," tuned it up (over and over again) and just about waxed the paint off it. Many a night, our faces outlined by the garage security light, we sat in it, fantasizing about the exciting and daring unchaperoned lifestyle we would soon know.

It had been agonizing for us waiting for his birthday to roll around, but it did, and now here we were cruising down Pleasant Avenue, windows open, elbows out, radio on, hood ornament fox tail flying. Unfortunately, it wasn't a long drive to school so we wouldn't be able to relish our new found freedom as long as we would have liked. Wes was all for skipping school; take a drive down to the shore or upstate; kept saying he needed to *get this thing on the open road!* And I'll admit it was a beautiful morning, beckoning us for all it was worth. Not being as brave as Wes (regarding skipping school) I asked him if he could just drop me at school first, before he set off on his excursion. Once aware he wasn't going to be able to talk me into it (although obviously disappointed in me) he decided to postpone his freedom flight. He would go to school as well—at least today. I was relieved, I didn't want to rain on his parade, but I didn't want to see him (or *me*) get in trouble. Couldn't *imagine* telling my folks I had even considered skipping school, let alone doing it!

We pulled onto the school property—on the road that ran between the school and the football field. We drove between the north end scoreboard and a group of students about to raise the flag. Last year's graduating class had donated a forty-foot-high aluminum flagpole to the school. We drove past them, searching for someone we knew who would notice we were driving. Over the small bridge and into the parking lot that I'd only viewed from afar. It was a gravel lot filled with the used relics of the working seventeen-year-olds, and a few brand new sedans (including an Audi!) given as seventeenth birthday presents to the kids from the Heights.

After third period I bumped into Wes in the hall and he told me he had an idea. I was already worried about what it might be. "C'mon, just a short outing. We won't be skipping the whole day. Leaving now is just like having a longer lunch. We'll be back by fifth period. How about it? Whataya think?"

What did I think of it? You can guess what I thought of it. I was afraid we'd get caught, and even if we didn't get caught I'd feel too guilty. Mom and Dad would never tolerate me skipping school—even one period. Just not the kind of thing you did. But Wes wasn't easy to convince. He let me know that while he sure would like me to join him, *he* was going! For the first time (and what would be the last) I allowed that just like other kids did all the time, I could miss one class, especially since it was going to be metal shop. Wes was glad. This decided we had to figure a way to get out of the building. The worst part was the awkward feeling while trying to stay hidden in the halls after the last bell had rung—the one that meant everyone had to be inside the classrooms. I'd never heard it from any place other than inside the classroom and at my desk.

I had told Wes *yes* but thought of and quickly apprised him of two possible conclusions to this act—hoping he might reconsider. It didn't work. He was committed. This was scary and I knew— wrong. We were practically tip-toeing—like in an old *Tom and Jerry* cartoon, hugging the walls—our shoulders rubbing against the metal lockers. After navigating the vacant downstairs hall alongside the gym, we snuck out a service door that opened onto the road by the edge of the football field. I could just feel the discovering eyes on my back; sure that someone had spied us, knew what we were doing, and was about to come running out after us. But no one hollered. Full speed now. *Making our break for West Germany.* Onto the track, over the bridge and into the abandoned parking lot.

In a flash Wes was in the car, door closed and engine running. He turned on the radio and I snapped it off. *Let's not be relaxing just yet.* Wes shook his head, disgusted at my lack of bravado. So far I wasn't having any fun; was real worried. We hadn't discussed where we were going or what we were going to do during this short fling. Out of the parking lot and over the bridge. I was sitting as low as I could (as if that would be any help). We were on the track now at the edge of the football field and approaching the big flagpole. After passing it we would go up the ramp to the road in front of the school building; the critical part. Being warm, almost all the school windows were wide open and I could see the tops of the heads of the students inside. *Could it be possible that not even one of them will look out the window?* We were in plain view, but thankfully no heads raised or turned. Apparently (miraculously) no one appeared to be looking out the windows.

I became aware of a level of confusion emanating from Wes, and I was hearing a strange noise, like a big screen door creaking shut. We were almost alongside the classroom building now, the one place we should be speeding up. But the car seemed to be slowing. I looked at the normally confident Wes whose face was now taking on a markedly dumbfounded expression. The strange creaking noise was getting louder *and the car was stopping,* though I had no idea why. I shot another worried look up to the open school windows. Instead of the students being bent over their desks, the openings were now crammed with wide-eyed faces.

And then it hit the ground, with an ear-crashing thud, right alongside the car. Six feet closer and it would have caved in the hood of the car. *The flag pole!* Driving by it the rope to raise and lower the flag had caught under Wes' door handle, and *we had pulled the entire flag pole down!* The adventure was over. Any hope the day had was over. I don't even want to talk about the afternoon and evening. The principal. The explaining. The police notification. The glances our friends gave us. And worst, *the terrible look of disappointment in my parents' eyes.*

CHAPTER TWENTY-ONE
On Being Prepared

It was another hum drum history class until through the fog of my day-dreaming, I realized the kid seated in front of me was turned around and whispering to me. And what was he saying? *"…did I want to come over to his house and study? Tonight? For the test tomorrow"?* My heart missed a beat, because this guy wasn't just any guy. This was Donald Webster, not the coolest of them, but a respected Heights resident. Every day he wore the neatest clothes—blue button-down shirts, maroon V-neck sweaters, gray flannel slacks, and white bucks. I would have given anything to be able to dress like that.

But why on earth would he want *me* to study with *him?* I certainly wasn't the "class brain," that was for sure. Lord knows a "C+" was an okay grade for me. And none of the kids from the Heights had ever invited me to their house, even for a *group* party. I was caught off-guard and flattered; in fact honored. While Don may not have been a straight "A" student, he never got less than a "B+." *What possessed him to think I could help him prepare for a test?* But, flushed and with no time to think of an excuse, I accepted. *I'd be over at seven sharp.*

I knew I'd have to do my afternoon paper route, but also knew I'd better find time to do a bunch of studying before I went over there, or I could be in for a real embarrassing evening. Three-thirty now. Papers will be here soon. Maybe I could get in a little studying before they arrive. Went to the bedroom, closed the door. No radio. This was serious. We weren't just talking about grades, we were talking *reputation*—and not just mine. I'd be carrying the banner for all the other guys on this side of town (Wes, and Rolly, and Vic). This could be an opportunity to gain an acceptance we'd never had. *Got to get to work.*

I read and turned the pages but kept finding my mind wandering. The information seemed simple enough as I read it, but a few pages later I was unable to recite any of the names or dates or places. *Nothing was sticking.* Finally, after coming back from a bathroom break, *at last*—a page made sense. Maybe we're getting somewhere. Then I realized the pages had flipped back while I was in the bathroom, and I was reading the same page I had just read three minutes ago! Shoot, there's my papers hitting the sidewalk.

Did the route in 45 minutes—a record for a Thursday, when there's an extra shoppers' section with all those inserts. The paper's too thick to fold; you learn to hate Thursdays. Pedaled the whole route standing up. Was back in my room at five-fifteen. If I didn't eat supper I would be able to study for an hour and thirty minutes. Unfortunately, so much for that idea. Mom and Dad didn't know how important my evening was going to be and made me join them at the dinner table.

Back in my room I was again frustrated at how I wasn't retaining information. *Boy was I in trouble. Don would rue the day he had asked me to help him study.* He'll know that not only do I live way across town, I'm not very smart. I was getting desperate and had to try a different method of studying the chapter, even though it would take more time. And I didn't have much time. I found a spiral notebook and put it on the bottom bunk alongside the textbook. (I was on my knees on the floor using my bed for a desk.) My plan was to start with the first paragraph in the chapter. Read it slowly and carefully, then slide the book away, think about what I had just read, *and then try to write the whole paragraph in just one sentence on the page in the spiral notebook.* If I had trouble remembering an important detail, I would allow myself one quick "look-back" for confirmation of a name or a date.

I tried it. I read hard, thought about it a minute, and then in my own words transcribed the main point of the paragraph into just one sentence in the spiral notebook. I read the second paragraph; thought about it a moment and then transcribed it into one sentence. Then the third. I was surprised to find myself making good progress. It was going pretty fast. (And I hadn't read the same page twice like I did before.) Ten done, only three more pages in the chapter. *6:30: I'm going to make it in time!* The chapter was finished and I had one and a half pages filled in the spiral notebook. I closed the textbook, got up off my knees and lay down on the bed. Notebook in hand I read every sentence, with the people named, the event, the date, and what it meant. It only took ten minutes to review the whole chapter. I was ready to believe I had most the main points. *Might* get away with it. Don might not see through me.

In the Heights and nervous. The large double-door entrance to Don's house was obscured until I was through the stone gates and past a high hedge and a line of blue spruce. I felt a chill as I drove my 41 Ford up the wide circular drive. I'd never been this close before, and knew I was out of my element. I was pretty sure I shouldn't park a blue and cream (okay—blue and *yellow*) convertible directly in front of this house. Better to hide it over by the garage. (Back on our street it didn't look so out of place.) Now or never, up the wide stone steps.

Don's parents were surprisingly pleasant. My arrival went much better than I had imagined. Two straight times now I had met Heights parents, and surprisingly both times they were perfectly normal. Inside, you should have seen the size of the rooms! There was a room that they called *the study*, where his parents recommended we go for privacy. Lots of wood paneling, and lots of I'll bet—real leather furniture. Books all over the walls. Not one, but two huge desks in the same room! We ended up sitting in two big easy chairs facing each other. *My mettle was about to be tested.* If I would have relaxed my jaws my teeth would have chattered.

Don said he'd start. He'd be the one asking the questions. My stomach knotted. I wasn't going to get any reprieve—in the hot-seat immediately. *Thank God,* Don started out with a simple question first. Maybe he was just being kind and didn't want to embarrass me right off. I held my breath waiting for the second question. Remarkably, I could almost visualize where he was in the textbook—halfway down page two, middle paragraph. Here comes another. *Luck was with me!* Maybe by the skin of my teeth, but I made it through. He finished the first half of the chapter *and I had made it!* Fortunately for me Don had asked manageable questions about the chapter's main points. I don't think he was good at digging deep for the small details. I was never so relieved and happy in my life.

He handed me his book and told me to have a go at it; ask him some questions. "Okay, sure." I found where he was and began. I was soon embarrassed, because after he had asked me the more obvious questions, evidently I had started out by asking more complicated ones. The evening went a thousand times better than I could have hoped for. Don seemed pleased. His parents seemed pleased. They even acted pleased just to have *met* me. But no one was more pleased and thankful than I was. We said goodnight and I was on my way home, singing at the top of my lungs, and giving thanks to the Lord for small favors.

History class was first thing after lunch. Don gave me a big thumbs-up as we sat down, though I wasn't sure that was going to do any good. Last night was one thing, but this was the actual test! My tuna sandwich was heavy in my stomach. Mrs. Payne's briefing was short. The exams were coming down the row. Soon everyone was bent over their desks. The only sounds were an occasional sigh or ruffling of paper. *Please God, be with me again.* He was. Listen to this: Mrs. Payne, who was known for her tough tests (you could never bluff through one of hers), had for once—finally made up one that was straight forward. For once, each question was in plain language and right at my level.

I was finished, and without having made a single check mark in the margin (which would've indicated I should go back and double-check that answer). *That was a first.* I didn't know if a few, or most of the other students had already handed in their answer sheets. But there was no sense going over mine. I knew I had already put down the best answer I could think of for each question. *May as well hand it in.* On the way to the teacher's desk, I noticed that except for a couple brains, half the class was still bent over their papers. Uh-Oh, that could be bad. *Maybe there are two pages of questions and I only got one.* She took my paper, checked it briefly, smiled, and nodded me back to my seat. That was that. It was over, for better or worse.

I could hardly believe it when the test scores were posted. I didn't just get an "A," I got every single question right! Don got a "B" again like he often did. My personal conclusion was, even though from time to time the teachers might goof and just make up an easy test, I was going to keep on doing my new spiral notebook procedure. Why take chances?

CHAPTER TWENTY-TWO
A Little Help With a Big Decision

Halfway through twelfth grade and best I can remember, very little input from my parents concerning what I might be doing after graduation. Certainly they cared—I'm sure of that, but I think they (and especially Mom) gave me more credit than I deserved for thinking ahead. Well sometimes I did—for tomorrow night or next weekend, but certainly not for a lifetime. I've finally recognized I almost never think far enough ahead, and this is just one more thing (and a big thing) I gave too little thought to. For me it was just another summer about to begin. Hard to believe I didn't realize earlier in the year—or better yet last year, that I was approaching a significant fork in the road.

And this was 1953. It wasn't a given that you'd be going to college. Most of our parents (on this side of the tracks anyway) hadn't gone. Their well-meaning advice dealt with trades, apprenticeships, or if such was the case—helping in the family business. Dad suggested that I might want to look into becoming a barber. He said they had it "made;" always closed on Wednesdays, only a half day Saturday, and all indoor work. Not a bad deal he had said, except you had to spend a lot of time on your feet. (Even as little as I knew or thought about a life's work, I was having trouble picturing myself as a barber.) To show that I *was* giving some thought to my future, I dropped some hints about maybe for just one summer—taking July and August off) and then in the fall, start my first permanent job, driving one of those big gravel trucks for *Sam Braen Inc.* You saw his trucks everywhere. Wes's dad told us that Sam gave all his drivers a big turkey for Thanksgiving. With nothing else to go on, this seemed as good as anything to make a career decision on.

By late spring the issue of my future did come up. And whenever it did I noticed Mom seemed concerned, to the extent I thought her eyes might be about to tear up. This made me suspect this point in my life might be more critical than I had thought. I always knew that Dad had dropped out of high school to work, but was surprised to find out early on, that Mom had been a high school valedictorian and attended Vassar college in New York; at that time just about the most exclusive women's college in the whole country!

Dad and I also discussed a handful of manly occupations, including factory jobs such as being a lathe operator, or better yet he said, a press operator (who earned even more). And no matter whether you were talking college or a job, there was one thing that all the guys were thinking about—especially the ones with older brothers; that "police action" thing going on in Korea! If you *did* make some plans and then the government up and drafted you, well that sure could mess things up. Sitting at a distance and overhearing Dad's occupational suggestions, I often heard Mom mouth the word "college." *College?* I hadn't yet considered that. No reason to. But if it was an option, it might be nice. It would extend my student role and postpone the really hard choices. But where and how?

Out of the blue, some direction. None of my doing, but a plan would begin to take shape. The previous summer I had taken a week off from my summer job to attend a Bible camp sponsored by our small Dutch Reformed Church. (The one out by the highway.) Everything about the experience—the woodland setting, the cozy cabins, my new friends, the nightly songfests around the campfire, were just great. Never a mean word. All *Golden Rule* stuff. And the counselors were neat; most of them students from a Christian college in Iowa. Now—almost a year later I received a call from "Digger," one of the camp counselors. He was a sophomore at Central Christian College and already knew what *he* was going to do with his life. He was going to be a minister. In fact he told me he had already registered for the fall of 57' semester at New Brunswick Theological Seminary. About as far ahead as anyone I knew had ever thought. *And now he was calling to try to convince me to go to Central.* With nothing else on the horizon I was willing to listen. And what a salesman, he made it sound just great. I never got to visit Central (or any other college for that matter) but as far as Digger was concerned, I didn't have to. He had more brochures and photos than you could have asked for. And neat stories too—of all the great things about campus life at Central. He gave me the phone numbers of some other Jersey kids who he was trying to convince, or who had already decided to go to Central.

We did our best to total all the costs, and came to the conclusion that it could be done. Between us, it was possible. I'd be able to pay the whole year's tuition using my savings and this coming summer's earnings, and my parents would take care of costs of the dormitory and meal program. For living expenses and spending money, I would just do odd jobs there at the college. *Roger Yahnke would be going to college in the fall!* No idea where I would be today if Digger hadn't called.

Here—as would luckily occur often in my life, I would be the undeserving beneficiary of outcomes greatly facilitated by friends, strangers, or events that presented themselves at a critical time; at a time when I was unaware of the necessity to be decisive and take prompt action.

CHAPTER TWENTY-THREE
Hugh School in a Nutshell

I waited a long time to say it (though by now you've probably figured it out). My high school days were *not* fondly memorable; not like what I've heard they're supposed to be. Certainly not like the TV series *Happy Days* (although my town, our high school, the kids and their parents, could well have inspired the series). We didn't have a dress code but didn't need one. Most the guys dressed just like Don Webster: button down collars, V-neck sweaters, gray flannels and white bucks. The girls (especially the pretty ones from the Heights) dressed the same just about ever day: white blouses, plaid skirts, saddle shoes, and ribbons in their hair.

Once again, I never mixed with those cool students. Probably my own fault; just didn't think I stacked up. Didn't try out for a team or a part in the school play, or join any of the clubs. Never visited the soda fountains after school, and even if I would have I'd never have had the nerve to sit down with any of those Upper Ridgewood kids. I was sure there was no reason they'd be interested in having me hanging around with them. And that made sense, because I knew I wasn't really one of them—not by a long shot. And *why*? Well besides the perceived caste system that kept me on the outside looking in, I was pretty busy. From seventh grade on I don't think there was ever a year that I didn't have either a morning or an afternoon paper route (or *both*)! And when I didn't have an after-school route, I had an after-school job; spent my whole junior and senior years stocking shelves in the Co-op on Godwin Avenue. Maybe that's one reason I never tried out for a team—would've had to leave practice early every day.

Now when I look back on it, I ask myself *why* was I always working? God knows it was no fun and I don't recollect the paychecks ever turning into neat things or any great times. I just thought it was expected of me—that I'd have to "chip in." Something you didn't question. I knew that Dad expected me to earn my own spending money. With my daily arrivals two minutes before the first bell and my departures two minutes after the last bell, I was doing my part to maintain a low profile. Never came close to being a participating member of the student body. Though most kids probably knew my name, they sure didn't know (or have any reason to want to know) where I was or what I was doing when I wasn't sitting there in class. My mornings remain a pre-dawn image of the alarm clock reading ten of five, and my afternoons of trying to wolf down one of those little *Mrs. Something's* fruit pies and an RC Cola before the papers arrived. Seems to me, all I did in high school was work. And this doesn't count Saturday mornings, when as you remember, by Yahnke tradition a son belonged to his dad to help with whatever had to be done. And with my dad there *was* something—always!

Well, I did one other thing: I thought about girls—wistfully imagining myself on a proper date with one of those popular ones from the Heights, or making up more daring scenarios with the ones that smoked and dyed their hair, and wore big earrings, and rode around in cars with older guys. These girls were sort of fair game to think about. I'm not so sure about those nice girls from the Heights. It worried me because I was pretty sure my friends didn't spend half as much time as I did thinking about girls. And I just knew the rich guys from the Heights didn't. But they didn't have to—they were *with* these girls all the time! As I look back (embarrassedly), it seems I spent most of my time thinking about female bodies. A key time was after I went to bed and before I fell asleep. *Real concerned about that.* But as far as real dates or going steady, nothing was ever put in action. No one would've guessed the extent of my waking hours' preoccupation. But I think I only had three dates in all my high school years.

Of the occasions I remember missing out on—being on the fringes of (or excluded from completely), few are more representative than my high school graduation ceremony. I'm sure that's supposed to be a landmark event; a reason for joy and self-indulgence and reckless acts. There's supposed to be parties and dances, lots of congratulations, and at least one big gift. I can only remember a few things about mine: A sweltering early evening outdoor ceremony; standing there squinting into a blinding setting sun—seeing only the silhouettes of the parents in the bleachers; and a two-second trip across a rickety scaffold platform to receive my diploma. *That's it.* I'm sure my parents were there; must've been, but don't remember any conversations with them, before or after the ceremony. I might have gotten one, but can't remember a graduation gift.

I do remember the rest of the night—lying on my back on the rear seat of Ralph Horlbeck's father's car, watching the streetlights go by as he and Skip drove around till 2 am, doing nothing, going nowhere. Next day it was over. Like for me it didn't even happen. I remember the envy I felt, when I heard that a bunch of kids from the Heights (*girls* included!) had rented half a motel down the shore, and were driving down—*to stay overnight!* Boy did Skip's dad have something to say about *that!*

The summer following my senior year would be like the preceding ones, except I knew I had to find a better-paying job (to be able to make a worthy donation to the college kitty). And I did get one thanks to Uncle Jim. He surprised us by phoning to say he'd found me a job working for a friend of his who owned a construction company. Although I'd say it was a "destruction" company, since we spent two months knocking down an old brick-walled building—mostly by hand! I was glad to have had the opportunity to earn some good money, but it was *not* a fun summer. I had to get up at 5:30 each morning, make my breakfast and lunch, and then walk a mile to the foreman's house to hitch a ride to the job site. What a ride. Dreaded it. I had never met such a pessimistic, complaining adult. Harold complained bitterly about everything, especially his wife and the boss. (And this transportation cost me five dollars a week!)

I was the only kid on the job. All the other workers were grown men, and from a breed I'd not yet met. They swore like you can't imagine, smoked all the time, never shaved, had bad breath, *and didn't wear underwear.* I knew this last item because once up on the roof ripping off scalding hot shingles, I was right behind a skinny guy who had a gaping hole in the seat of his pants! And they drank on the job, and were always telling each other about their sexual escapades, the likes of which I had never heard and could scarcely believe. I vowed that whatever I ended up doing in life, it would *not* be something that would cause me to associate with these type individuals on a daily basis. Having now experienced my first permanent job, I knew it was pure good fortune that Digger had given me that call about Central!

CHAPTER TWENTY-FOUR
The Best Kept Secret Ever

I can't remember how or if I initiated the application process; I wasn't even sure it was what I wanted to do. Never consciously made any decision on my own, just responded to the requests for information. The process (thankfully) seemed to pick up speed on its own, and then *Bingo*—it was a done deal; without me ever having considered myself responsible for the outcome—neither pulling for it nor fearing it. This was my first experience being the recipient of a fortunate unfolding of events over which I could have but failed to assert myself. Shamefully I admit that there would be many more times in my life when I would undeservedly be the beneficiary of these perhaps destined evolutions. In any case everything for college just fell into place.

Early August 1953 found Digger and I and two other Jersey recruits standing on the curb in front of his wood-sided 47-Ford station wagon. When the last photo, hug, and "yeah, don't worry" seemed to really be the last, we seized the moment and clambered in. It took a while to get situated, the car being full of borrowed suitcases, boxes and plastic bags. The engine caught, some final nervous waves, and we were off for the flat, corn country (though I for one had some second thoughts, praying I had not bitten off more than I could chew). Had no idea what requirements I would be faced with or what treatment I would receive as a college freshman. (Although based on my summer employment, I was sure it was going to be better than what I would have sampled as a member of a hardened work force.)

Went straight through—22 hours. Sweating in the day, cold at night. No car radio. No space to get horizontal. But it was a small price to pay for what would soon unfold before my eyes. When we rounded the final corner and the campus was in sight I was greatly relieved. It wasn't threatening, not in the least. In fact, it appeared wonderfully hospitable, even better than the brochures. Just what one would ideally hope for: expanses of bright green grass, old ivy-covered stone buildings, large oak trees, tiny arched bridges, and a network of brick pathways, one leading to the brand new dorm I would be staying in. I had an immediate good feeling about what I saw and was anxious to be a part of it.

I'd never sampled the culture of the Midwest; never met anybody from Iowa, or Wisconsin, or Minnesota (and evidently they had no reliable information on us). New Jersey in those days—to these farm kids, was almost a foreign country, so we were regarded with a flattering curiosity. We were jokingly referred to as the "east coast hoods" and received more attention than we were accustomed to (or deserved). Half the male students here in Central were enrolled to be Dutch Reformed ministers and their father already was. I realized this could be a new start. *I could be anyone I wanted to be!* No one here from Ridgewood High. No one aware of my mediocrity. I could even act like one of those kids from the Heights. If I started right away I could talk to *anyone*. Just get up the nerve and *do it!* If I was ever going to have a chance, it would be here. I felt safe and poised to break out here at Central Christian.

During freshman orientation I got an idea. (Actually I had this idea for years.) *I needed a cool nickname to assure my new persona!* Roger just didn't seem like a very experienced name. No one knew me here except Digger (who obviously had previously gotten into this nickname thing). So this might be the perfect chance to change my moniker. I wanted something short and cute, maybe just one syllable. I made up a list and then spent a goodly amount of time in front of the mirror, mouthing them out loud. Finally, and none too soon—two hours before the "Let's Get Acquainted" party, I made my final selection: *"Dink!"* I would be Dink Yahnke. Sounded cool to me. Could hardly wait to hear it shouted in my direction. I was excited visualizing the moment when after waiting in line, the lady at the Welcome Desk would ask me for my name. As calm and naturally as I could, I'd tell them *"Dink,"* like I'd said it hundreds of times (which I almost had). Then I'd watch them scrawl it on my name tag and stick it on my lapel—marking the official beginning of the new me!

There were only three or four freshmen between me and the registration desk. *Only minutes from a fresh start.* Some other freshmen who had already been through the line were standing together drinking cokes and chatting. Among them was a handsome athletic-looking guy from Wisconsin who was going to be our star tailback. He and all the other football guys had arrived a couple weeks earlier to start practice. Everyone seemed to know and like him, and I have to admit he appeared to be a really nice fellow. One reason I liked him was because he was only as tall as I was. It made me feel good when short guys were popular. True, he was more muscular than I was, and I'll bet he never lifted weights—leastways not as hard as I had. And he wasn't stuck up; in fact he was genuinely friendly. When we'd pass on campus he would always wave and smile, even though he didn't know me. His name was Dwayne Krentz. I could see he was going to be one of the "big men on campus," which was okay with me.

The girl in line in front of me turned and began making small talk, including the fact that she had gone to the same high school as Dwayne, and that they were good friends. She confirmed that he was every bit as nice as everyone said. And then *she asked me what my name was*. I was caught off guard. I hadn't prepared myself to mouth my new name until I was officially asked for it by the staff at the welcome desk. But I rose to the task, took a quick breath and told her that *while my real name was Roger, everyone called me Dink*. A look of disbelief spread across her face.

"Dink? That's impossible." I had no idea what she meant. What did she mean—*impossible?* She pointed at Dwayne Krentz—almost urgently. "That's Dwayne's nickname! Dink!" She explained that as a child when he pronounced his first and last name together it sounded funny. So they started calling him that. "Look! Look over there. It's already on his name tag." Incredibly, she was right. I could see it from where we were. The expression of disbelief on my face outdid hers. I was in shock, foiled by a one in a million coincidence. *Back to the drawing board*, and not much time either. I'll say not enough time; try as I might, after reviewing all the runner-up names, when asked by the woman at the Welcome Desk, I replied, *"Roger."*

In spite of no cool name college was a new and uplifting experience. I was accepted at face value (even more) and was pretty much (God knows why) regarded as someone to know and say Hi to. I would have liked to do what I had to, to stay that way, but never knew what that was. The school was located on the edge of a small Iowa town that had been settled by immigrants from

Holland. Being Dutch was almost a prerequisite for residency. The phone book was full of "Vander-this's" and "Vander-that'ers." In front of every store were wooden boxes of tulip bulbs flown in from the Netherlands. Every road into Pella boasted a sign reading *The Tulip Capital of the USA*. Of course there were only four roads into Pella: one each, directly from the north, south, east and west. I'd noticed, out here (unlike north Jersey) all the roads were arrow straight and crossed at ninety-degree angles.

The town center was a one-block-across, tree-shaded, grassy park, with brick walkways, wood benches and an ornate white gazebo. Everyone called it the "square" and it was the starting point for directions to anywhere. The four streets bordering it boasted seventy-five percent of the businesses in town. One of interest was an old board-floored, soiled and bone-bare place where dairy farmers brought in milk to be tested. The movie theater was only nine seats wide; five on one side of the aisle and four on the other. There was a farm equipment dealer, among whose inventory of dinosaur-like contraptions I could not find one whose function I could figure out. Half the population lived on farms. As a result, one of the first big surprises for me—something I never saw in New Jersey, it seemed every tenth guy you passed had at least one finger missing.

Each morning started with a short chapel service that had an amazingly good turnout. Of course that made sense, since almost all the students were from good Christian families, and at least half the male students intended to make the ministry their life's work. *And believe it or not, I was toying with the idea myself!* Just thinking I might finally have a plan was exciting. I had three or four classes each day, which left me half the day to study or just waste time—even take a nap after lunch. It was hard not to feel guilty with such an easy routine. I was quite sure my family was envisioning a much more demanding lifestyle.

I was assigned the newest all-male dorm and had a surprise the first week. The dorm father was a minister from town. His son Joshua—the student leader for the dorm, had organized a co-ed party!(One of the few I would see on campus.) The party started with a game of charades. He lined up a row of girls, the first with her face against the wall, the second facing back towards the room, the third face against the wall, the fourth facing back into the room, and then three more face against the wall. The lineup complete, Joshua spins around and asks the group, "Well what is it"? Obviously he was met with silence. Finally he had to explain. "It's the William Tell Overture!" More quizzical looks. And then Joshua explained, "Rump, Titty, Rump, Titty, Rump, Rump, Rump!" This remained the most risqué event I experienced in my whole time at Central.

Mom had recommended a liberal arts curriculum, so that's what I signed up for; not even sure what science or business majors were available at Central. They obviously had a religion major (and everyone had to take *Old Testament History*). Mom had said that you could do just about anything if you got a liberal arts degree, but I would learn that this was one time when Mom wasn't exactly right. To me the classes seemed just like high school; not harder or more complicated (which concerned me a bit). No problem with grades—was doing better than in high school, and could have done even better if I would have studied more.

I wasn't convinced the courses I was taking were practical or moving me at any speed towards a life's work, but all the other guys seemed to be taking roughly the same courses. Guessed it would all fall in place later, and since I was doing okay academically I decided to just enjoy it and hope for the best. Everyone ate in the one school dining hall—a large, fresh, clean, pastel-walled room in the basement of the girls' dorm. About thirty tables, all with white tablecloths. And the food was great! Oh, one other thing about Central: *there weren't any kids here from the Heights!* No "beautiful" people. No privileged souls. Have no idea where or how these Midwest kids grew up, but they sure turned out okay.

I mentioned previously that for spending money I would do odd jobs at the college. Of these, my favorite was the late-night cleaning of the gym. After the final floor buffing and being the only soul in the building, I would turn on all the lights full bright, dribble down the shiny court, juke the last defender and shoot a lay-up (to the roar of the imaginary crowd). Almost gave me goose bumps. Even with this part time working, my classes, and studying, I had plenty of time left over to do whatever I wanted. And again, the best thing, *it seemed everyone on the campus really liked me.* I sure was happy Digger had gone to the trouble to give me that April phone call.

My beefy roommate had a plan for himself that he thought may as well include me. He cajoled me into going with him to the Athletic Office *to sign up for the football team!* Can you believe that? *Me on a football team?* (Although I was the heaviest I had been in my life—142 pounds). The fact that I was a born-small, destined-to-be-small person, was something I fought all day, every day. To better wage this battle, at the age of fourteen I'd begun lifting weights regularly, which did make a difference, although certainly not substantial. Some of my kinder friends used to say things like: "C'mon Rog tell us what you're doing for your pecs?" If they were being truthful, maybe the coaches would notice and consider me (if they didn't recognize my lack of gridiron acumen). They did let me on the team but the smallest helmet I could find still swiveled on my head. I made all the practices and once they even put me in a game! I was scared and confused and knew I didn't belong out there.

And there was an even worse athletic involvement. One of the linemen, a big guy nicknamed "Tank" took me under his wing. He thought we guys from *Noo-joy-see* must have all belonged to gangs and had lots of fights. More than the others he loved to refer to us as "hoods." But Tank was a boxer and this led to trouble. In a soon to be regretted effort to impress Tank, I mentioned Dad had been a boxer. This was not an outright lie, Dad did have a punching bag in the cellar, and I think he did spar with some local fighters. But the real mistake was adding that I'd had several amateur fights. (This *was* an outright lie.) You should have heard Tank's response. There was no getting out of it. He was taking me to his gym, and I was going to be on his team! No way to avoid it. (*My darned play-acting again. Trying to be something I wasn't.*) I ended up being put on the roster without ever being asked to spar with any of their fighters.

My first fight was at the KRNT theater in Des Moines. In its cold cellar I viewed the others in my weight class and was shocked at how much bigger (and meaner) they looked! Checked the card and found my opponent was going to be Marcus Rivers. Found him. He and his manager were going through a routine. The manager would shout, "What'r you gonna do Marcus"? And Marcus would shout "Kill him"! They just kept repeating it. God, I was shaking. And Tank (if you can believe this) seeing this told me to walk over and stand right in front of the door with my back to them, purposely blocking their view of the arena.

Do What? Obviously couldn't do that. The fight came off and it was an embarrassing showing on my part. Out of justifiable self-defense my only weapon was the left jab. Between rounds the club manager asked me what in the hell I was doing with just those left jabs. I told him I was 'feeling him out'. He hollered, "You feel him out with a straight right to the mouth"! *In the third round I thought I might have an excuse. I felt a sharp pain in my left knee, only to realize it was the first body part to hit the canvas when he downed me.*

Really surprised they would entertain it, but Tank's club scheduled me for a second fight that fortunately I didn't make. I was on the Central track team. (Only because no one had tried out for the pole vault I was solicited and ended up a completely untrained and lousy pole vaulter.) No one was assigned to teach me even the rudiments and I didn't ask for any help. I just practiced the same lame attempts on the far side of the field, a good distance and almost out of sight of the few coaches we had. On the day of my scheduled second fight, we had a track meet. On one vault I didn't have enough speed at the end of the run, so the pole faltered at the vertical. I was stopped dead, short of the bar, feet up and going nowhere. I let go and landed on the hard packed cinder runway *on a locked-straight left arm,* dislocating my left elbow. Never told the track coach. Never went to the infirmary. It ballooned in size like a *Popeye* forearm and went on to turn several shades of purple. It was a heck of a price to pay, but I had a reprieve from that night's scheduled ring appearance, and my collegiate boxing career was never resumed.

With little or nothing to do in the evenings, several of us were allowing Digger to drive us around in his now famous 47 Ford station wagon. It was November and cold and the heater didn't work. Realizing we were just wasting gas and tire tread, Digger suggested we return to the dorm; after a quick stop for our usual cheeseburger and French fries. Enroute, Digger became aware of the too-frequent use of the "F" word emanating from the back seat, and let us know that he was not comfortable hearing it. In our defense we explained that it was doubtful we could communicate effectively *without* using it. Digger—realizing our plight, suggested that instead of using the actual "F" word, each time its use was deemed necessary we just use the word "fork." If we said "fork," while he would know what we meant, he could tolerate that.

Inside the diner we took our seats at the counter. I think perhaps the sauciest looking young woman I'd seen in the state of Iowa was the lone waitress; false eyelashes and dyed red hair falling onto large breasts (doing their best to escape from a low-buttoned light green smock). Wow! She came over to where the four of us were lined up (all eyes fixed on her and just a little short of mesmerized by our fantasizing). She asked us for our order. We all responded with the standard "Cheeseburger and French fries."

A short time later while munching away, I noticed Digger was using the diner-supplied large toothpicks—with a plastic bow attached, to stab and raise the French fries to his mouth. Like with me they kept falling off and down onto the counter. Not only had I seen his problem, but our provocative, bedroom-eyed waitress had evidently also noticed the toothpicks weren't doing the job. She sauntered over, put her elbows on the counter in front of Digger, leaned forward with her face directly in front of his, looked into his eyes and said, "You wanna fork?"

CHAPTER TWENTY-FIVE
Something New! A Girlfriend!

My second year of college was even better than my first year. Didn't try out for the football team and certainly didn't mention anything about being able to box; just enjoyed my courses and my still-great spare time. And I had one brand new leisure time activity: *Going Steady!* At Central every girl either acted just like your sister or actually *was* one of the other guy's sisters. In the dorm at night there wasn't much gossiping about Central's co-eds. If they weren't somebody's sister, their father was a teacher here, a minister in town, and likely had graduated from Central. My freshman year had involved only two or three dates—attending completely harmless school sponsored activities, such as hayrides (in the daylight) and square dances (with as many faculty members in attendance as students). But this second year was going to be a lot different.

By the end of the first semester a certain Minnesota farm girl and I had become Central College's favorite twosome. Constance (who her very close friends could call "Connie") was a straight "A" student—which you would suspect, seeing her in the library with her horn-rimmed glasses sitting next to a pile of reference books. My guess is she would have been the answer to any mother's prayers; smart, proper, and seemingly always above the fray. While at first glance her apple pie and gingham freshness may have suggested a naiveté, anyone tempted to pull the wool over her eyes would learn she was not to be messed with. Everybody looked up to her and wanted to be where she was, including the boys. It seemed she had just picked me out. I knew I was lucky and went along willingly. It was a first for me, associating with someone who with just momentary eye contact knew exactly what I was thinking, and then passed a proper and sometimes humbling judgment on it. It was as if I had surrendered to someone, and I kind of liked it. Constance was a junior—a full year ahead of me. It was understood that she was smarter than I was and frequently (usually) took charge of our activities.

Knowing Central—with its daily chapels, mandatory Old Testament classes, and parental faculty, the physical nature of our relationship stayed pretty much at the *holding hands* level. Each night after our stint in the library I'd walk her to the front steps of the women's dorm to say goodnight—in full view of the dorm mother and a dozen other couples. Before college broke for the summer I began trying a more intimate parting gesture; sealing it with a kiss—as best I knew how. *How complicated could it be?* Well my attempts were certainly kisses, but they didn't look like the ones in the movies, and they weren't stirring my soul or my loins. (I prayed it was better on the other end.) It was a little embarrassing when one of the nearby couples began really going at it. To me, the sounds and movement accentuated the inadequate and perfunctory nature of my attempts. But we had time and I was pretty sure Connie wasn't ready for that stuff.

I knew little about these kinds of relationships but was beginning to think that ours could well be the beginning of something serious; very possibly a long-term relationship. One tip-off of this (another first for me) was the sadness I felt when we parted for summer vacation. And Connie gave every indication she would miss me just as much. We both agreed that our August reunion couldn't come too soon and it would be wonderful.

CHAPTER TWENTY-SIX
A Fork in the Road

Not sure when it first crossed my mind that I should interrupt my college career. *Not a pleasant thought.* But during the summer I'd been doing some thinking. Two years of college under my belt and I couldn't shake the feeling I was getting ahead of myself. Still no major; was accumulating credits but no idea at all about what life's work they were pointing towards. And I didn't have an inkling of a preference for some profession. Might be that I needed a break—some time for things to hopefully fall in place (again).

And compounding this issue there was a very good chance I would be drafted before I finished my senior year; maybe even before I finished this coming year. The Korean War had only been over two years and the "Cold War" was going full swing. Most of the country thought the Russians might launch missiles at us any day. Kids don't realize it now (with the current *All-Volunteer Army*) but back then if you weren't "married with kids" you were probably going to get drafted. *And that was me.* So if I *was* going to be drafted, maybe I should beat them to the punch—volunteer and be able to choose my own poison. And I did have a plan. God knows why I thought I might like to be (or would be qualified to be) a pilot, but that's what I was thinking about. It sounded kind of glamorous. It would keep me out of the trenches and satisfy my four-year military obligation.

First week of July I decided to check it out. Made the drive to the old Post Office in Paterson where the Air Force recruiters had their offices on the second floor. Tarried a moment in the lobby, realizing I might be getting ahead of myself. *Well I'm here, probably can't hurt to get a little information.* Climbed the dusty steps to the second-floor landing, where a grimy paned window was allowing some sun to filter into an abandoned hallway. The place was deserted. In spite of no activity, halfway down the empty hall I saw a floor to ceiling wall mural with four gleaming jets in formation. *Yup, that's what I was thinking about.* Walked down to it, took a deep breath and turned towards the door. It was locked! The Air Force recruiter wasn't in! My brave day was foiled. End of plan "A," but with no plan "B" I started down the scarred wood-floored hallway—head down on my way out, but not to any place I had yet decided upon. Then almost to the opposite landing, *What's this?* A small two-sided easel on the floor said *"FLY NAVY."* It displayed a young couple on a balcony at the edge of a large body of water. He was wearing a Navy bridge cap and had a pair of gold wings over his pocket. Outlined on the horizon was a large ship. *A what, an aircraft carrier?* While standing there deciphering this message my arm was taken by a smiling naval officer. I followed him into his office and told him why I was there. He gave me a quick once-over and started the questions:

"You got two years of College?"

"Yes Sir." Small lie. I had skipped Music Appreciation and was two hours short of the required 60 semester hours. (I would fix this by taking an elective course at a local community college.)

"How about your vision, do you see 20-20?"

Could tell the truth here. "Yes sir"

"Five foot seven?"

"Yes Sir." (First time in my life I was ever proud to be five seven and a half.)

"Well, you're eligible. You just have to take and pass this test."

Next thing I knew, I was at a desk taking a long test; the likes of which I had never seen. It covered just about every discipline I could think of. One interesting section showed a complicated cardboard box, all flattened out. The question was—what those pieces would look like if reassembled. Surprisingly (and thankfully) it seemed easy to do the required construction in my head, and I think I got most those right. Many of the other questions weren't objective. It was like they were trying to find out what kind of guy I was. For example, one question was: "Where is the clutch on a Harley Davidson?" I think I knew but wondered: *If I put down the right answer, will they think a guy who rode motorcycles was too reckless to be a pilot.* Would it be better to play dumb and miss that one on purpose?

Completed the test and evidently did well. Signed more forms and that was it. Somehow with a mission of "just getting information" *I'd gone and done it!* Next stop (in two weeks) would be Floyd Bennett Naval Air Station in Brooklyn—to be officially sworn in! Lucky I didn't have an accident on the way home. I couldn't wait to share the news with someone. (This was way before cell phones.) I knew this was a very big thing I'd just done, *maybe the biggest thing ever.* It was the most excited I had been in my life, although this excitement was tempered by *"Now I won't be seeing Connie in August!"*

Two weeks later on my drive east on Route 4 towards the George Washington bridge—to New York City and Brooklyn specifically, I passed an empty field with a crudely painted sign: **Airplane Rides Five Dollars.** I was still worried about some lurking deficiency resulting in the Navy withdrawing their offer; for example they might ask me if *I'd ever been up in an airplane?* Up till now the answer was "No." *Better to be prepared.* Pulled over, paid my money and went for a ten-minute open cockpit ride. It wasn't exciting. I certainly didn't discover the one thing missing in my life. Things on the ground seemed to look normal, just as I would have expected them to look. I was able to keep track of where we were and I didn't get sick. It was an unemotional, matter-of-fact determination, but my conclusion was (assuming I could learn to properly manipulate the aircraft) *I would be able to do this flying thing.*

The afternoon at Floyd Bennett went pretty good; passed my physical exam—though not without a hitch. Discovered I'm one of those people whose blood pressure can really go up when excited. (Something that would cause me problems in the future.) But, along with one other Jersey kid and one from Long Island *I was sworn in as a Naval Aviation Cadet!* All the way home on the long drive to west Jersey, I couldn't help repeatedly glancing down at the large manila envelope on the seat next to me. It was stamped "OFFICIAL ORDERS" and contained the authorization and details of my pending travel to Naval Air Station Pensacola, Florida—the *Annapolis of the Air!*

It was the first week in November before I actually made the trip to Pensacola. My arrival was delayed by a recruiter's ambitious plan: assemble a cadet class all from Texas, to be called "The Texas Rangers". They had been one short and their class was going to be filled by a New Jersey Yankee—*named* Yahnke! No one knows it now, but then—in 1955, old people in the south (and as far west as Texas) were still embittered by the actions of the Union soldiers. And evidently they made sure their grandkids heard all about it. My Beaumont and Galveston peers didn't just *know about* the Civil War, it seemed they were *still fighting it!* I had studied it in American History but am embarrassed to say I had no idea it was still such a divisive event. There were a couple guys (Jim Skinner from Amarillo, and Allan Yatsko from McAllen) with whom I initially feared for my safety. I had a real challenge turning their suspicion into tolerance, and finally into acceptance. Thankfully that did happen.

The "Texas Rangers" (Class 41-55) was one collection of wide-eyed, "all ears" students starting their Preflight Training. It would be sixteen weeks in a classroom before we would even see a cockpit. We had a comprehensive curriculum, including a thorough review of geometry, algebra, and trigonometry. For me (with Mom's liberal arts curriculum), it could hardly be called a review; more aptly—a "Crash Course!" There were also courses on Terrestrial Navigation, Celestial Navigation, Airframes and Power Plants, Combustion Theory, Water Survival, Military Law, and a variety of P.E. (Phys Ed) courses. In class, it sure got your attention when the instructor would start his presentation with "Gentlemen, what you will learn today could very well save your life."

Our class like all the others had a Marine Drill Instructor in charge. Remember the film—An *Officer and a Gentleman,* with Richard Gere as the cadet and Louis Gossett as his "DI." Our DI controlled our every movement, marching us to and from everywhere, including classes. Once inside he would stand against a side wall checking for any drooping heads. When he saw one, he would shout out, "Son, that's what the Marine Corps issues you *night* for—sleeping! Now stand up!" (Guilty cadets spent the remainder of the class standing.)

A little more about my two new Texas friends: In Preflight there were monthly "Smokers," boxing matches pitting cadets from one battalion against those from another. Jim Skinner (who you will hear about twice more) was our heavyweight. Jim—lanky, squinty eyed and square-jawed, appeared to be made of 50 feet of pressure treated 2x4's, his fists hanging like cinder blocks, knocked out every opponent in the first round. (And some things aren't fair, not only was Jim of imposing physical capabilities, he was also "smarter n' hell!")

My other Texas friend and the most loyal "Texas Aggie" I would ever know, was Allan Yatsko (the McAllen guy). He was a chisel-faced rebel with dark hair, gray eyes, and a five o'clock shadow by noon each day, and my roommate for the whole of Preflight. Hearing them every night I quickly learned all the words to Allan's two favorite songs: *The Streets of Laredo* and *Ghost Riders in the Sky.* In violation of the strict rules against it Allan had gotten into the Naval Cadet flight program while married. and would be successful in keeping this fact a secret for eighteen months (and the only one I knew who did manage to pull this off). While he drank, smoked, failed to avoid fights, and played poker until all hours of the morning, he was "true blue" to his wife the entire time. One day I saw him shaving *without* shaving cream and commented on how much that must hurt. He responded in his emblematic coarse base tone, "Hell man, I usually knock them through with a hammer and bite them off from the inside."

Not sure if it was just these guys or a statewide thing but being side by side with them (and the other "Rangers"s) for sixteen weeks, I developed a great respect for Texas pride. Jim and Allan were great examples of those wind-hewn men off the prairie (although in the years to come, flying would not treat either of them kindly). These two guys, myself, and I guess about 90 percent of us made it through Preflight, but not without demonstrating the most common failings of guys our age. I was much surprised (and flattered) to read in the glossy tri-fold pamphlets in the Visitors Center, that I, along with my peers (who all seemed like me—very average if not measurably flawed), represented *"the cream of our nation's youth!"* From what I saw I wasn't so sure, but I was willing to give the pamphlet the benefit of the doubt and hope they were right.

CHAPTER TWENTY-SEVEN
Visiting Connie and a SERIOUS Happening

I'd only been in Florida for six weeks when mandatory Christmas leave was announced. My first break from Preflight Training was upon me before I was ready for it; before I could feel as if I had earned it. But that didn't mean I didn't have big plans. *On the way home I was going to visit Connie!* It had been six months since I'd seen her and although I must admit I had found very little time to dwell on the relationship, I was excited about the thought of this reunion. On this final midnight leg to Minnesota I was thinking about her family; trying to imagine what her mom and dad would be like, and their farm, and her little town of Grand Meadow. I'd only have three days there before continuing home for Christmas. At least for the moment I was content with my decision to have left college early. I was proud to be making my way in the world; especially on my way to becoming a Navy pilot. No longer just another student wandering a campus. I was older now and I was doing something patriotic. And to make sure this fact would not go unnoticed by Connie and her mom and dad, I was wearing my uniform—or selected parts of it that I liked best and had combined in a completely unauthorized fashion.

It was only my second airline flight. My first one being two months ago when I'd flown down to Pensacola to start flight training. The Navy had set that one up whereas I'd arranged this one myself. And it wasn't simple. I had to change planes in

Atlanta and then Chicago, where I boarded this late-night flight to Rochester. The aircraft was a DC-3, a two-engine, propeller-driven aircraft that had been a real workhorse in the military (called a C47). It carried about 30 people, although on this midnight trip the dimly lit cabin contained only a handful of dark and shadowy passengers, and no flight attendants (which was kinda spooky). It would've been even better if it served a hot meal (or any meal), or have carpet on the floor (or a whole lot more insulation). *My feet were frozen.*

The flight was "IFR"—"Instrument Flight Rules" the whole way (which means the aircraft is inside the clouds with no visual reference). It had been snowing like mad when we left Chicago and the pilot said it would likely be snowing in Minnesota. Hard to tell now—pitch black outside. We were scheduled to arrive about 1 a.m. Not a great time but I didn't have any choice. There weren't a lot of flights into Rochester. I told Connie I'd call her when I got in, and they would drive the thirty miles to pick me up. As we started our descent, I snuck back to an icy metal toilet to take a nervous leak and double-check my appearance (on the outside chance Connie *would* be there when we arrived). And this particular DC-3 must've been a military aircraft because the bathroom walls were still painted olive green.

Back in my seat I heard the gear come rattling down (which grinding sound seemed to confirm the plane's age). I strained my eyes into the darkness outside, expecting to see the city lights of Rochester. *Whoa!* Jerked my head back—startled; the landing lights were switched on and total blackness was instantly converted to blinding white. The strong beams were suddenly reflected back by a wall of snow streaking over the wing and past us. No chance to see anything now, and knew this weather would make the approach and landing a little difficult.

If I would have known now what I would later learn, I would have been worried. In spite of prohibitively bad weather conditions pilots have often succumbed to something called *"get-home-itis."* This is aviation jargon for a captain's insistence on getting the airplane on the ground when low ceiling and visibility make a landing attempt inadvisable. Pilots are most apt to do this to avoid missing their anniversary dinner or their daughter's ballet debut. The urgency of these planned activities persuades them to descend lower than they should have (below "Published Minimums" for the approach). This infraction is the main cause of those fiery night-time accidents a mile or two short of the runway. Fortunately I didn't know about that yet. I just knew airlines were professional and pilots flew all the time, in all sorts of weather—and surely must know what they were doing. Till we landed I would occupy myself visualizing the great reunion that was about to start.

In spite of the poor visibility the pilot made a smooth approach and good landing. After a long rollout we turned off the runway (the *only* runway) and started taxiing in. Must've been slick, as I could feel the pilot constantly tapping the breaks, which caused repeated hydraulic squeals from below. Couldn't hear it but could imagine the dry snow creaking under the tires. Peering out through my window I still could see no lights or even shapes. Came to a halt in front of what I guessed—as the only building on the airport, had to be the terminal. Emerging from the aircraft I scanned a 360-degree tree-lined horizon; no buildings, no lights, not even likely silhouettes. It was as if we were an alien ship that had set down in a completely snow-covered, remote pasture, miles from civilization. The stairway railing was an iced rope. I felt the hairs in my nose freeze on the first inhalation. No vehicles in sight. Zero activity. Not even a slight glow in the sky to indicate the location of some nearby city. Hard to believe we could be anywhere close to the city of Rochester. The terminal building was the only structure in sight, *and it didn't look anything like a terminal.* It was a long barn-like building with wood siding and a shingled roof. We hurried towards it as best we could on the slick packed snow.

Entering from the ramp and a few steps inside, I saw nothing more than an expanse of raw gray concrete. The interior was barren. No kiosks. No desks. No tables. Not a stick of furniture anywhere in the room. The opposite wall had a set of glass-paned double doors that probably led out to the curb and pickup area. There was no ceiling—you could look right up through the trusses to the underside of the roof boards (where some trapped birds were darting about). Glancing to the left and right, at each end of the building I saw what I guessed were ticket counters; unmanned with no equipment or displayed materials to indicate they were ever functional. Connie wasn't here. Would've been great if she would've been, but the plan was that I would call her when I got in. (Still, she *did* know my scheduled arrival time.) I called her number and she picked up on the first ring. She sounded excited (*thank you Lord*) and said they were on their way. Everyone else had already been met or had hurried out on their own. I was the only passenger left in the building. In fact, except for one distant figure now raising up from behind the counter at the far left of the building (and the birds in the rafters), *I was the sole living thing in the terminal.*

The building was heated, but just barely—had to keep

moving just to stay warm. Kept expecting to see more people, at least *somebody*—like a janitor, appear from *somewhere*. They never did. There was no music, no TV, no PA system. The only sign of recent commercial activity was one wire newspaper rack (completely empty). And it wasn't that all the shops were closed at this late hour, there *were* no shops! No shoeshine booths, no newsstands. Since the four inside walls were also the outside walls, there were no doorways or halls. This was one very weird place! I was beginning to feel like I was part of a Rod Serling's *Twilight Zone* episode.

With a half-hour to wait for Connie, I decided to get the ticket for my return trip. Not hard to figure out where to try. There was only one other human in the terminal. He was standing motionless behind the counter on the far-left wall, surrounded by darkness. One hanging overhead light illuminated his head like a marble bust in a museum. Had on a dark suit; should be an airline employee—hopefully a ticket agent. I crossed the desolate space and presented myself in front of his position. My voice barely registered in the large silence. (Hadn't spoken a word for three hours and no time to clear my throat first.) "Good Evening." He didn't look up, but I continued anyway. "I'd like to purchase a ticket from here to New York, La Guardia. Leaving on Thursday the 17th." He seemed to start doing the right things; pulled a stub out of a drawer, flipped through it adjusting the carbons, and started writing with a ball-point pen. (This was way before electronic ticketing.) Face up again, but expressionless, he spoke: "Your name please."

I began, "First name, Roger." And then knowing the difficulty in trying to spell Yahnke just from hearing it, I told him that I would spell out my last name. When I saw he was ready, I began:

" First letter: Y... Second letter: A..." *Got no further*. After I said "A" the agent glanced up from making the entries and eyed me strangely. (And I can tell you, this place was strange enough for me, *without* running into a nut.) After a second or two of sizing me up, he looked back down, apparently ready to start again. I continued, "Third letter: H..." His head came up again. His expression was a mix of confusion and suspicion. *What the heck was his problem?* We were surrounded by silence and could have been the only two living souls on the planet (and I'll bet—certainly were the only two within five miles.) He tentatively returned the pen back to the name block on my ticket, ready to make the next entry. But this time he kept his eyes fixed on me. I continued, "Fourth letter, N." With that—for some reason that must have done it. He laid the pen down and took two steps backward from the counter (out of arm's reach) never taking his eyes off me. During this awkward standoff, I happened to notice the brass name plate over his pocket. It read, "YAHNKART"! *He thought I was the nut!* The first four letters of my name being the same as his, he thought he some crazy passenger was buying a ticket using *his* name.

I would like to have told you it was, but it was *not* a great three days. It could have been. Lord knows I *wanted* it to be. We took some short walks, watched some late night TV, and visited a couple of her high school friends. All that went okay. Her mom was nice—real nice. Her dad? Well he was different. Seemed to me he was overly cynical, particularly when it came to my military status. A couple times I think he went out of his way to say something "to get my goat"—unnecessary belittling things. Hopefully it was just because he wasn't ready for his daughter to be getting serious about some guy. I don't know. I hadn't given him any reason to dislike or disapprove of me. In any case I never felt comfortable with him. He was a big man, and one time (perhaps I shouldn't have been wearing my uniform) he took my small-sized hat and plunked it on top of his large, wavy gray-haired head. The hat looked absolutely ridiculous, like a piece of doll's clothing. It made me think, *if my head was that small, how small must the rest of my body look?* The evening of my second day, he asked if I would like to join him for chores the next morning. Ever since my morning paper routes I've hated early get-ups, but you can bet I said "Great!"

I was up and ready to go at first light. And I was a real trooper—up to my ankles in manure, wet to my armpits milking, having my teeth rattled on the back of his feed cart. I was wholly and vigorously involved, lifting barrels, shoveling grain, and tossing hay. I went at it like it was my own farm. Anyone arriving on the scene would have been hard pressed to tell which of us owned the place. It was a matter of credibility. He already knew I was from New Jersey and that wasn't in my favor. In view of what I thought had been a great attitude and a laudable effort, I was surprised (and disappointed) when later at breakfast, he jokingly—but only *half*-jokingly, described my contributions as *what you would expect from a city kid.* That hurt, but it was far from the worst thing to happen on my last full day in Minnesota.

Talk about surprised. Talk about shocked. I was caught completely off-guard and reduced to befuddlement. That evening at a quarter to eleven, inside her tiny house, lying on a throw rug on the cold board floor in her living room, next to an old gas heater (and only fifteen feet from her parent's bedroom door!) this wonderful young woman, the light of her mother's eye, *wanted to have sex!* I was numbed, struggling to believe what was about to take place. Sure, this is how these things end up, eventually—I think. (*I know.*) But I never thought about *when* it would come, or where it would be. At Sunday School and from my folks (God knows from my mother), I'd heard it a hundred times: *A girl saves herself. She waits until she's married.* And Connie? God sakes, Connie! Other girls maybe. *Other* girls, but not Constance Luedeke, with her thick glasses and long-sleeved, high-necked blouses.

But there were no two ways about it. She had decided she was going to give up her body tonight! And from the way she was talking and wildly undressing, she wanted me to take it in the next two minutes! It was like she had suddenly thrown all caution to the wind and was going to do it right here and now. I couldn't help feeling as if I was the one who was going to be her partner, not because she wanted to seal our love across the miles, but merely because I happened to be the one present when she made her decision. I don't know. What I do know is—*I wasn't ready for it,* not by a long shot. I might have been out on my own, my own man in many respects—planning vacations and buying my own airline tickets, but I guess there were a few things I wasn't doing, like spending time with working girls, never considering that they might "want it" too. I was twenty years and two months old, but had not yet lost my virginity. Sure, I *thought* about it a lot. In fact fantasized a great deal more than I felt was normal. But I hadn't been *doing* anything about it. This would be my first time, but oddly enough I wasn't preoccupied with that aspect. I was concerned about everything else! At the bottom of the list was any possible physical pleasure that might be in store for me. I was in no way mentally prepared for this. But there was no altering the course of events she had scheduled. *I was going to have to perform, and soon!*

What followed was probably the most awkward, most unskilled, and most unsuccessful effort ever devoted to satisfying a woman. True, I think I started out okay, nuzzling her and stroking her now exposed female body, nibbling and kissing her. I did all those things which I was almost sure would have been expected of me, and pleasurable to her; though to me they seemed to be artificial, forced, contrived, mechanical motions. Finding myself in this situation, with its definite requirements and larger-than-life expectations, I was *not* feeling confident. And why? Well after a goodly time of conducting the before-mentioned activities, irrespective of what Connie might be feeling, I was aware of a frightening numbness precisely where I should have felt some spreading activity. And worse, I had no reason to believe that five more minutes was going to suddenly make any difference. An even greater fear began to overtake me. I knew I had to consummate this act. *I had to.* I was striving and straining, pleading to the gods of love-making and swearing under my breath, beseeching myself with desperate urgency. *C'mon. C'mon. Please! C'mon.* But not a bit of progress where I needed it.

I had never considered such an actuality. This lack of arousal was in stark contrast to the daily if not hourly (and often untimely) erections that had plagued me from the time I was twelve! God knows I had spent more time than I should have thinking about being in this exact situation. In bed at night I'd made up exciting scenarios, such as myself and some voluptuous woman—captured by the bad guys, handcuffed together, the length of our bodies unavoidably pressed against each other. And every time—in a matter of minutes (if not seconds), I'd find myself in possession of a hardened device that demanded satisfaction.

Due to my lack of readiness I had to delay "going for it." I continued to position and reposition, avoiding and postponing. All the while my pretty Connie lay there, twisting and anticipating. I looked down at her—head back, eyes closed, mouth raised, and cursed myself. Embarrassed and ashamed, and becoming more so with every minute, I prayed she was not aware of my difficulties, and that some miracle would occur. Some minutes later we were a mass of tangled clothes, elbows, perspiration, and floor burns—with me in no better condition. I could have cried. I was ready to scream. I could have wrung it off and stomped on it. With jaws clenched tight lest I fill the air with profanity, I was now wildly distraught. I tugged her this way and that, transmitting stupid instructions (when I was the one who needed help). I got her to allow me to slide a pillow under her hips, which some guy had told me positions the woman's pelvis just right. (As if the previous angle was part of the problem!) But she did it. She was going to try anything to get this thing on the road. She tugged it under her full white buttocks, wiggled a bit, and indicated she was ready. *God, if I just was!*

Almost impossible to imagine I was not overcome by her warm, damp body, and round, heavy thighs. I wasn't infused with the slightest lust or desire that I knew should be consuming me. I was just a man with a mission—his own project, totally dedicated to overcoming his inability, wholly concerned with it; a preoccupation that left no room to savor the moment and let nature take its course. I lessened the touching and kissing I had been doing. How could I continue without being able to consummate it? And for sure Connie didn't need any more foreplay. Her movements and moaning indicated she was ready for ignition. If she would have had further physical arousal (in addition to her gritty determination to cross this bridge tonight) my lack of performance would have been even more devastating. (If that's possible.) I was exhausted, discouraged, and greatly chagrined.

The mental anguish, futile contortions and flailing about was abruptly interrupted by a resounding loud metallic clang! My heavy navy brass belt buckle had struck the base of a metal floor lamp. With the sharp noise reverberating in my ears I could visualize her father (in the next room) bolting upright in bed. Like a boxer in the throes of a hopeless loss, I would be "saved by the bell." *This was going to be my reprieve*. I scurried for distance in mortal fear that any second the bedroom door would be yanked open and I'd be looking up at her father! Connie must've had the same thoughts, as out of the corner of my eye I saw her arms up and several articles of clothing all in the air at the same time! Any pending activity was going to be curtailed.

I was quite sure in the days to come she would spend a fair amount of time reflecting on this non-event. (I knew I sure would.) I was afraid that after this, my male attraction would never be the same, never have the same allure. And I was right. The big fade began soon afterwards. From down in Florida—with letters, flowers, telegrams and phone calls, I tried desperately to win her back. She had begun dating another guy at college. I knew him; an older guy there on the GI Bill. He'd been in the army, been overseas, smoked, drank, and almost immediately seemed to have some kind of mysterious hold on her.

I didn't know when or where (or with whom) a similar opportunity would present itself, and I was deeply concerned about its outcome.

CHAPTER TWENTY-EIGHT
What I Remember About Flight Training

Christmas with the family was great or as good as it could have been (the memories of my Minnesota visit all too vivid). New Years day I was on my way back to Pensacola and Preflight training. Happy to say I never fell asleep in class and passed all the tests. Earned ninety-eight dollars every two weeks and had money left over. No car; rode with other guys or hitch-hiked. Spent many a Saturday night at the infamous Trader Jon's in downtown Pensacola; one night earning a bottle of wine for my guys by winning a pushup contest. Cadets were not allowed to go ashore in "civvies"—ever; a regulation made to be challenged. Proud as we were of our uniforms, we all had at least one set of craftily hidden "GQ" togs. It was the preferred attire should you choose to go drinking or slumming. This way, if you passed out or were arrested you'd not visibly damage the reputation of the U.S. Navy.

Everything went fine, minus my Minnesota memories. Not sure if the hurt was in losing *her* or just in *losing*, but it hurt! It was the first time I'd felt this helpless. I spent valuable time and energy trying to win her back, including imploring a college buddy still up there, to make a personal appeal for me. Occasional false hopes. One night after a wrenching phone call—head down and with mounting desperation, I went out into the pine grove behind the barracks. There, standing on a bed of needles, looking up through an opening in the treetops, I pleaded for help from above. *Please God, give me some sign that you hear me, and that it's in your hands.* No sooner had I gotten the last word out of my mouth than the opening above me was sliced in half by the searing white trail of a meteor arcing across the night sky. This caused a level of excitement I could barely contain, though time would show it was just a capricious celestial coincidence. Came close several times. She would cry and say things that made no sense. Then it was harder to get her on the phone. Finally not at all. I never saw Connie again.

A certain military custom caused me to frequently miss getting fed! For the sake of optimum eye appeal in parades, individuals are positioned by height—from the tallest to the shortest. This way there's very little difference between the tops of any two side-by-side heads. As you might suspect—at five-foot seven and three-quarters I was third from last. We marched everywhere in this sequence. Arriving at the chow hall for meals I was number 37 in a queue of 39. Since our formation was allotted only fifteen minutes to accomplish this eating exercise, I frequently found myself just starting to load my tray when the DI shouted *"41-55. Fall in! Now!"* But then a possible reprieve: Halfway through Preflight our DI announces he has recognized this inequity in the order of eating and is going to alter the formation. "From now on gentlemen we are not going to fall in by height. We are going to start lining up alphabetically!" *I was now next to last, just Allan Yatsko behind me.* Thank God for those small Kellogg cereal boxes—the ones with the perforated flaps in the bottom. I could fit one in each pocket and sneak mouthfuls all day.

When I finished Preflight Training I was transferred to

Whiting Field. There at last, the books would take a back seat to flying. Here cadets underwent twelve weeks of actual airborne training, culminating in the first and perhaps most revered entry in any pilot's log book: *"Cleared for Solo."* I got mine, although not without a discouraging realization: There was an aptitude for flying, or a confidence that some guys had, that I was not blessed with. I had to do each maneuver over and over again, forcing myself to memorize the sequence and force of control inputs that were required. Ultimately I was able to have the plane performing on cue, although I knew it was a result of no natural ability; just the fortunate result of playing back a series of memorized mechanical actions. I doubted any of my friends were having the difficulties I was having (or if they were, they weren't talking about it).

And I didn't get through without paying my "worrying dues." I had a good friend named Jack Pulcheon who we nicknamed the "Animal" (due to his resemblance to the hulking, uncouth American prisoner in the hit film *Stalag 17)*. My friendship with the Animal created one aphorism for life: *nothing is ever as hard to do as the guy who just did it tells you it is!* At the end of each phase of flight instruction and before advancing to the next phase, cadets had to demonstrate a competency in all the flight maneuvers taught thus far. Except for a few unconsciously bold and confident souls, these "check rides" were rightfully dreaded. Animal was a week ahead of me in the syllabus so always underwent his check rides first. His terrifying narrations of the untaught maneuvers he had to accomplish and the unreasonable expectations of the check pilot, caused me more than my share of sleepless nights and nauseous mornings.

As a youngster I had a minimum interest in aviation; never

built model planes and couldn't tell you about any aviation movies I went to. So when now introduced to it, many aspects of it were a first-time revelation. I was especially impressed by the "fail safe" systems built into cockpit design. One such neat thing: If a pilot is coming in to land and has forgotten to lower the wheels (yes that does happen) approaching the runway, when the aircraft gets below a certain speed (but well prior to touching down) a loud horn begins blaring in the cockpit. Upon hearing this unmistakable warning the pilot realizes his forgetfulness and quickly puts the gear handle to the DOWN position. *Neat!* Well you'd think so anyway. A cadet friend of mine, Ron Meyer—on his first solo flight made a "Gear Up" landing (forgot to lower the wheels). This is the faux pas of all faux pas as a pilot. Usually wrecks the airplane and since the spinning propeller strikes the concrete, usually ruins the engine as well.

During the accident investigation one of the tower controllers testified that he saw Ron's wheels were not extended and was shouting this to him over the radio—*that his gear was not down.* In fact he did so all the way to the scraping, spark-showering touch down. The chairman of the Accident Board hearing this, looks at Ron and asks, "And Cadet Meyer, why did you not heed that call!?

"Never heard it sir. There was this loud noise in the cockpit blocking everything out."

Graduating from Whiting I got someone with wheels to help me move my few things the thirty miles to Cory Field, where the next two phases of training, night flying and instruments would be accomplished. At night there is no visual reference to assist the pilot and he can easily become disoriented. To avoid this, a pilot must be able to interpret and rely on his flight instruments.

That's why the Navy schedules Basic Instruments *before* Night Flying. You cannot fly at night by looking out the window (as was tragically demonstrated by John Kennedy Jr.—who exposed himself to the pitfalls of night flying before any instrument training).

Basic Instrument flight training lasted about two months. One could move on to night flying only after passing one of those dreaded "check rides" for the Instrument phase. This time even worse than previous check rides, in that it was conducted "under the hood." You had to wear a large visor-like device on your helmet that blocked the sight of anything outside the cockpit, thus simulating being engulfed in clouds. In the case of some cadets also inducing vertigo or career-ending claustrophobic reactions. You had to convince your check pilot that using only your flight instruments, you could keep the plane straight and level. Or after being flipped over on your back, using only your instruments you could get the darn thing right side up again.

Instrument flying was sufficiently challenging to cause some cadets to improvise (cheat). They would add padding inside the top of the helmet to cause it to ride higher, then put the visor hood on at a slightly canted angle. This altered positioning provided a slight space under one side of the hood where they would be able to get a "sneak peek" outside the cockpit. I considered this a bad idea and did not participate. The Instrument Flying phase would account for more "wash-outs" than any other phase of training.

Finished with Instruments we started night flying training. On dark nights cadets would joke that *they felt like they were in an ink bottle, inside a coat pocket, hanging in a closet.* Before going up on a night flight we were first required to observe a night takeoff and landing pattern. The night I was scheduled, myself and a dozen guys were taken to a plowed field about a half mile from the runway. The night landing pattern was "closed circuit," meaning the aircraft never left the landing pattern. Our assignment was to watch and memorize the pattern size and spacing. We viewed this as a not too valuable pastime, mostly carrying on other conversations.

The Officer-in-Charge however, viewed the session as being very important and was intent on us not leaving until we had one thing down pat: the various exterior lighting modes a pilot would select if he had an emergency, but no radio to transmit his problem. The most critical of course was if your emergency was an engine failure! The exterior lights signal for this most dire emergency being *all aircraft lights full bright and flashing.* Not long after this had been explained to us than the Animal points to an aircraft on the downwind leg—with all its lights full bright and flashing, and an aircraft that did not appear to be maintaining altitude. Jack grabs the Officer's shoulder, points, and says "Like that? That guy has his lights full bright and flashing!"

The instructor being alerted, looks up—ready to explain away whatever, and then observing the plane; yes, a plane was in fact on the way down! *We were going to witness a crash as part of our familiarization.* The aircraft used for night training was a "built like a brick shithouse" prop plane called the T-28. We didn't visit the crash site, but learned that even after it had taken out trees, bull-dozed a hundred feet of dirt and shrubbery, skidded another hundred feet along a concrete culvert, and then flipped over onto its back, the sturdy airframe remained intact, allowing the cadet to unstrap and drop to the ground—*without a scratch!* An emergency vehicle standing by was immediately dispatched to retrieve him. Its occupants—as always, a cadre of super-motivated, tattooed bodybuilders hustled him aboard (according to the cadet later—"threw me into the truck") and peeled out, sirens on and pedal to the metal. Halfway to the base hospital the driver flipped the vehicle over. Checking into the hospital they found the cadet to have contusions of the face and head, a broken left arm and collar bone.

This emergency vehicle ride and later personal experiences have taught me that calling an ambulance (manned by overly enthusiastic paramedics) can be chancy. My recommended procedure is: (1) Phone 911, (2) before they get there have someone put you into the back seat of your neighbor's Lexus, (3) meet the ambulance at the Emergency Room entrance.

Next, Saufley field for formation flying; either two planes flying together—a "Section," or four planes—a "Division." After a combat loss, you've probably seen the "Missing Man" formation at the memorial service. It's where just three aircraft fly by. The most common type of formation flying (used at air shows) is called "Parade." In it, the second and other aircraft are on a precise 45-degree bearing off the lead airplane. The best way to know when you had successfully maneuvered your aircraft onto that 45-degree bearing would be when—to your line of vision, the wingtip light of the plane ahead, was superimposed over the head of the pilot flying that aircraft. Once this "sight-picture" was achieved, geometrically your plane had to be on the required 45-degree angle. All you had to do then is *join up and stay dangerously close*.

I viewed this formation phase of training as downright dangerous. Piloted by cadets as untrained and unproven as I was, were jockeying their aircraft within a few yards of each other! While most of the other cadets appeared to be up to the task, I recognized early on that formation flying required a certain visual perception and motor skills that I did not come by naturally. While I graduated okay from this phase of training, it was my conclusion that there had not been a single day when due to my own lack of skill, I had not narrowly missed colliding with another aircraft. (Most misses due to a hugely fortunate last second correction!) I don't think my friends were aware of my deficiency.

Since this phase of training was conducted at a remote field, transportation (having to hitch a ride to and from Pensacola) was a real drag. The recruiter had advised against bringing our own car to Preflight, so I had not brought my "like-new" shiny black 1941 Desoto. It was a real "beaut;" a never used, garage-kept old car that I had spent many an hour washing and waxing. I was sure it would be a collector's item someday; a car I would bring to those *classic car* shows. But for now—down here, to gain the required mobility (and be better placed to do some dating), I needed wheels.

Accompanied by several cadet friends (who opined it would be to their advantage if Roger Yahnke had a car) I set about checking Pensacola's used car lots. Midafternoon I found a really cool car: a coral and cream 53' Mercury Monterrey hardtop convertible; the type of car that any young lady would like to be seen in. However I was seventy-five dollars short. *Where would I get seventy-five dollars?* As if it was the kind of thing everyone did, the guys said I should just ask my father. *Ask my Dad?* Only after their insistence, for the first time in my life I asked my father for money. I phoned him and *couldn't believe it—he* said yes! And though it took a few days, he wired me the money via Western Union. The car was mine! Maybe my dad was mellowing in his old age. (More about this transaction later.)

Next stop Barin Field. Forty miles away just across the Alabama border. The one unique and revered aspect of being a Navy pilot (not available in the Air Force), is being a *Carrier Pilot*; having landed on board one of those flat-tops—eligible to be a member of the now infamous "Tailhook Association." Here I would undergo the training to prepare me for a carrier landing; six weeks of sweating it out before the day I'd fly out over the Gulf of Mexico and try my luck aboard some WWII carrier. That day I'd need to make five successful "traps" to earn my carrier rating. "Trap" is the word used to describe a carrier landing, in that your tailhook catches a wire, abruptly yanking you to a stop. If you landed long and missed the last wire, you would not be able to stop. You'd skid over the bow, brakes locked, and plunge down 50 feet to the water. Then while slowly sinking the ship would churn over you. If you landed too short you stood a good chance of hitting the stern ("spud locker") of the ship; an impact which would mark the end of you and your aircraft.

Landing aboard a carrier is no easy task. In addition to the perils of landing too long or too short, if you landed off-center— too far left or right, the arresting wire would whip you sideways, collapsing the gear and seriously damaging the aircraft. It is the epitome of aircraft control. Unlike landing on a long runway where your touchdown point and speed can vary considerably with no adverse effects, in a carrier landing (for the reasons just stated) you absolutely must touch down at a precise location and be at a certain minimum speed. Day after day we cranked up our SNJ aircraft for simulated carrier landings, using a grass landing strip on which a carrier-sized, rectangular touchdown zone was outlined with white lime.

To assist pilots in making their carrier landings (here in practice and on the actual carrier) the Navy utilizes a Landing Signal Officer. This experienced carrier pilot stands abeam the intended landing point with arms outstretched left and right—each hand holding a brightly colored paddle. He adjusts his arms up or down as necessary to signal your deviance from the optimum glide path. (It worked but has since been greatly augmented by a high-tech optical mirror system.) This fellow also graded our landings to be sure we were progressing; getting better and better until we were consistently touching down halfway between the beginning and ending lines, as well as halfway between the side lines. This phase was as challenging as formation flying and accounted for almost as many "wash outs" as instrument flying.

To improve the chances of having smooth air, carrier landing practice was conducted right after sunup (before the ground could heat up and cause convective turbulence). This meant for us—now in November, it was still dark when we got to the ramp to start our preflight inspection (with a flashlight). Some mornings it was still below freezing, and it was necessary to use a piece of thick rope to scrape the frost off the wing's leading edges. (The airlines don't use rope, they spray the surfaces with hot alcohol.) You *never* take off with any ice or snow on the wing surface. It changes the *shape* of the wing and thus changes the amount of lift it can generate. (There is a serious aircraft accident every winter as a result of this.) The whine of the starters and the sounds of back firing usually coincided with the first pink glow in the eastern sky. We referred to our ungodly early wakeup time as "O-Dark-Thirty."

Purportedly for security Barin field had an all-night Duty Officer. One important early next morning duty was to wake each cadet scheduled for the early first launch. As the D.O. I couldn't bring myself to just snap on the ceiling light and shout. Instead, I'd jostle his shoulder until I got a worthy response. Since it was recognized that a cadet might fall back to sleep, a second duty was to make a "ten-minute-later" re-check of the room—to ascertain the cadet was indeed up and dressing. One morning when making this re-check I *did* find cadet Burnham back asleep. I did my shoulder shaking again—more vigorously, till he rose up and swung his legs to the floor. Sitting on the edge of the bunk, head down, one hand scratching his tousled hair, he nodded okay and motioned me to leave.

I was relieved of duties not long thereafter and strolled down to the chow hall for some scrambled eggs and bacon. No rush, you weren't scheduled to fly the day after you did the all night duty. By coincidence the route back to my room took me back past Cadet Burnham's room. Glancing into his well-lit room I was shocked to see him sprawled on the bunk. Checked my watch— only twenty minutes till his scheduled launch! *Wow! Don't know if he can make it.* Hollered in loudly, then went in; physically pulled him upright while urgently tapping my watch crystal two inches in front of his face. Now wide-eyed he recognized the critical nature of the situation and understandably panicked. He was a blur scrambling for his clothes. No time for socks or brushing of teeth. He was out of the room full speed, into the hall, still trying to poke one hand through the flailing arm of his flight suit. His only chance would be a dead run to the flight line. Back in my room I laid down for a doze.

About nine, my roommate came running in to tell me about a fiery first period crash. One aircraft in the pattern had flown into another (like I was afraid I was going to do during the Formation Flying phase). They both went down in a tangled metal mess. The pattern altitude for Carrier Qualification is flown so low there's no chance to bail out. Both cadets were killed. The plane that had flown into the other was piloted by Cadet Burnham.

In spite of unnerving training diversions such as just described, I completed the Carrier Qualification training and *the big day arrived*. I had not slept well and had more than my share of butterflies. My flight plus two others were being briefed for the flight out into the Gulf. This was the flight we had all awaited; the one where we'd get our five shipboard traps and be qualified to call ourselves *Carrier Pilots!* The mood in the Ready Room was cautious and quiet. (Didn't see any of those overly confident cadets I had mentioned earlier.) This check ride would be different from all the rest: *We had never actually done what we were going to be asked to do.* Our practice sessions were just semblances; nothing like what was about to transpire.

And there was another problem; one that wasn't on anyone's list and shouldn't have been: *Time!* We were going to have enough of a problem with the landings without being told we had to get them done in a hurry! This seemed to be the main concern of the officers organizing the flight. They told us we had to get out there quick, set up quick, fly a tight pattern, not waste any time. The USS Saipan would only stay out there for one hour and thirty minutes! You either got your landings in or you didn't. Computing it in my mind: three flights of four aircraft equal twelve aircraft, each needing five traps. *How are we ever going to get sixty carrier landings in ninety minutes!* And to make things worse, my flight drew the short straw. We were to be the third (last) of the three flights. And the Yahnke curse, I was the fourth (last) aircraft in our flight. If we ran out of time, I was the one that was going to get screwed!

The trip out went okay. Approaching the ship the first flight descended to the pattern altitude of 500 feet MSL. The second flight held at 1,500 feet ready to drop down to pattern altitude when the last aircraft in the first flight had his fifth trap. My flight was orbiting at 2,500 feet, stuck there until the second flight was cleared down to pattern altitude. My heart was racing. It was surreal from above, looking down at the daisy chain of miniature yellow airplanes over the bright green water; strung out on the downwind leg, turning base, on final, and hitting the deck. And there were plenty of sound effects; non-stop throughout this continuous loop the LSO (Landing Signal Officer) was screaming instructions and condemnations over the radio. I watched the planes hit the deck and be yanked to a stop, or hit too long and miss a wire; looked like most of them were getting the first five they attempted. *Please God help me when it's my turn.*

Being the last aircraft in the last flight I was very concerned about time. Since I had not marked our arrival time, I was at a loss as to exactly how much time we had remaining. I did know we were well into it when the first flight completed theirs. Big shuffle now—musical chairs in flight. The second flight was now descending to the pattern altitude of 500 feet, while we descended to 1,500 feet. The first flight climbed to orbit at our just vacated altitude. This took a good five minutes. Finally, after what seemed like way more time than it should have taken, the second flight completed their landings, and our flight was cleared to pattern altitude. One of the guys turned left instead of right and we lost another few minutes trying to again align ourselves. *Finally—* we were set up in the circuit. Number one's already on final. Number two was turning base. Number three was halfway along the downwind leg, and I was just entering downwind. Hooray! First's got a wire! He made it. Second guy's on final. Number one off the bow, airborne. Number three on base. As number four, I was almost to the base position.

Turning it I made the required call, "Gear Down, fuel 1200 pounds." During fleet operations pilots have to make this fuel quantity call so that the ship can set the resistance in the arresting wires to be right for the total aircraft weight. Number two is getting unhooked. He made it too. Three on final. I'm right behind him. I was experiencing an exhilaration I had not yet come close to sampling. Even in this incredibly focused maneuver I was aware of the clean blue sky, the expanse of emerald water beneath me, and the clean—sweet smelling, fresh air. For these carrier landings, our cockpit canopy was slid all the way back—an open cockpit! It was an aura of being in a very special place at a very special time. I filled my lungs and squeezed the grip on the stick.

The ship underway at fifteen knots left a pure white foam trail in its wake, that I was now just lining up over. Wings level. Altitude okay. Didn't know exactly what my control inputs were, or why, or where my eyes were looking, but somehow the plane stayed lined up and was descending at just the right rate. Shoulder harness locked. Airspeed… *about ten knots too fast*. Little power off. Little nose up trim. Double check the gear. They're down. Off center. Gotta slide a little left. That should do it. Looking good.

What's that? The LSO was screaming something at me. Couldn't decipher it. Words but no meanings. Still had good paddles. Felt okay. Ship looming up. I'm under control (I think) but I'm going to hit harder than on land, but that's how it's supposed to be. Ship under me! No green. All gray. *Wham! Kerunch!* First the impact noise when the tires pounded into the deck and the wheel struts compressed, and then the screaming ratchet whine as the arresting cables were pulled out. Head snapped forward. Helmet hit the dash. Hand slipped off the stick. *I got a wire! I've made a carrier landing!* It was then I realized another voice was screaming at me. *Oh yeah, gotta reduce the power so the wire can pull my aircraft back until there's enough slack in the wire that it drops off my tailhook.* They're indicating it's out. Add power. Take off! *Number One* was behind me on final, about to touch down. If I didn't get back in the air in two seconds, they would have to give him a "Wave Off" (deny his landing attempt) *because I was in the way!* This is called a "fouled' deck" and the *last* thing you want to do is be the reason your roommate doesn't get his trap!

Somehow I made my second and then my third, and then—a monkey wrench in the plans. A wind direction change, meaning the ship had to change course. (Carriers always turn exactly into the wind before recovering their aircraft.) *Another five minutes wasted.* We had to just orbit until the ship was established on its new course. *This delay could do it. I may be screwed!* Back in the pattern. On the downwind. Turning base. On final. Made it! Got my fourth! One to go! *Just do it one more time.* Climbing out off the bow, lowering my left wing for the turn to downwind I heard the words I'd been dreading: *"Flight Three—everybody. Rendezvous at 3 point 5 overhead. That's it. We're all through."*

I was ill. We were going back and I'm one trap short. Could've done it; *know* I could have, but didn't get the chance. On the return flight I couldn't stop shaking my head and could hardly muster the strength to make the normal radio calls. The elated voices of the other flight members were in stark contrast to my depressed state. The flight to shore was one of the most discouraged fifteen minutes I had yet spent. I didn't cry but felt that I could have. What's worse, once back on the ramp you should have seen the carrying on—all the back slapping and congratulations. It was just one big celebration all the way to the hangar. Except I was not part of it.

Back in the hangar the instructors debriefed the flight, but with no indication of future plans for me. No mention of when I might be rescheduled. I was assuming I'd be dropped back to the next class; lose a week (or two) and go out with them when they went. I wondered whether at that time I would only have to get one trap, or do the whole five again. I'll bet the whole five. Unable to remain silent and needing some consolation I shared my great disappointment with Alf Rylander—a close friend from Preflight who was part of the flight. Seemingly surprised he answered "Whattaya mean, not qualified?"

Evidently he hadn't been counting my traps. He wouldn't have known that I only got four. I told him, "Only got four Alf, I was in the upwind turn when they cancelled the period. We ran outa time before I got to shoot my fifth. I was screwed by that hour and thirty thing."

"No way. We all qualified. Look at the blackboard."

What? All, he thinks. I knew I only got four. Afraid of what I might see (yet praying Alf was somehow right) I weaved my way through the desks towards the blackboard, waiting for the annotations to come into focus. *Could they possibly have not noticed? Could the instructors have lost count?* Lo and behold I *was* checked off as a completion! To this day I'm not sure if they knew I only got four and just figured I would have made it on my fifth try, or if *I was the one* who lost count, and *did* get five. In any case, regardless of the reason I was now a full-fledged carrier pilot and that was a recorded fact; one that could never be challenged or revoked.

As you might imagine, there was a great celebration at the Cadet Club that night. The place was rocking. The Fats Domino hit *Blueberry Hill* had just come out and was being played on the juke box every other song. I don't know if I'd ever felt so relieved, so elated, so euphoric from any single day's accomplishment. And coincidentally, this historic deed was accomplished on December 7th—the anniversary of Pearl Harbor. I wanted all my family and friends to know (and wished I still had a certain Minnesota farm girl to tell). Got a pocket full of change, found a pay phone and called everyone I could think of. Unfortunately, only once did I get someone on the other end—my sister Laura, and although I'm sure she failed to grasp the scope of this accomplishment she did manage to sound excited at the news.

Carrier Qualification was the last phase of Basic Training and I was finished with it (and a little proud of myself). In one week I'd be off to Corpus Christi, Texas for Advanced Flight Training, and *jets*! In the few days off before departing I decided to catch a flight up to Jersey and personally bring Mom and Dad up to date (okay, brag a bit). I got into La Guardia late but got home okay and got a good night's sleep. Over breakfast I filled the folks in on my training prowess. When finished, anxious to pay my respects to my beautiful 41' Desoto, I went to the garage; eager to sit in it and admire the neat dash, old radio, gray felt upholstery and feel the steering wheel in my hand again. But the garage was empty. Had Dad let Hank take my car? I met Dad coming out of the house and asked him. He looked at me like I had said something stupid, and replied, "Where do you think I got the seventy-five dollars for the Mercury?"

Advanced training had the same segments as Basic Training: *Instruments, Night, Formation,* and two new ones: *Tactics* and *Gunnery*—all done in jets! And once again we were pretty much overwhelmed. You'd think I would have had some memorable flight experiences to relate, and I'm sure I did, but to this day the actual flight training in Advanced is a too-fast, gray blur of briefings, flight lines, more classes, studying for tests, worrying about check rides and frantically asking each other for tips on how to pass them. It was as if I was a steel ball in a pin ball machine the whole time—ricocheting crazily from bumper to bumper until finally tumbling into the bottom hole. Graduation! Just hard to recount that journey.

I remember more about what little free time we had, catching an hour at the pool, discussing the latest hit songs, girls, and cars. I particularly remember (maybe because I was in cowboy country) Marty Robbin's "A White Sport Coat and a Pink Carnation." It was a Playboy anniversary and the barrack walls were plastered with centerfolds of voluptuous creatures (that I may have snuck more time in front of than most guys). These images provoked their share of evening searches. On the rare occasions when I did get a female candidate, the next day I was not at all anxious to reflect on the details.

It was a hot time for American cars—specifically the big Olds 88 Rocket with the first wrap-around windshield, and the new 57 Chevy Impala with its great sweeping tail fins. A month before completing Advanced, I one-upped the Chevy Impala and Olds 88 by purchasing a 1955 Thunderbird; aqua with a white leather interior, whose future collector's value I failed to anticipate (congratulating myself two years later for having sold it for almost the same price I paid for it). My second day as a "T-Bird" owner I parked it in the grass lot in front of the Cadet Club and went in for a beer (and to make sure everyone knew about my new wheels). After a couple cold ones and having spread the word, I was ready to consider an evening on the town. A bevy of envious young pilots followed me to the front steps to take a look at my T-bird. I was more than willing to honor their requests for an appropriate turf-slinging getaway. Turned the key, revved the engine a couple times and popped the clutch. And it *was* memorable. From beginning to end—*the two feet it lasted.* In my excitement to exit I had failed to recollect the details of my parking, and was unable to see the two, 18-inch high, chain-connected concrete posts I had pulled up against. While the damage was not extensive, the incident was sufficiently embarrassing to cancel my plans for the evening; plans to visit one of the local "body exchanges" (where with my new wheels, the chances for a favorable outcome would have to be improved).

June 1957. At last, a certified Naval Aviator. I had completed Advanced Training. Done! Whatever that would mean. Since Advanced was all in jets, I was not only now a qualified pilot, but moreover—a qualified *jet* pilot! (At this time, a still small and esteemed group.) A graduation ceremony was held at Naval Air Station Kingsville, Texas—in a small town right next to LBJ's ranch in the town of Alice (where records indicate Lee Harvey Oswald stopped on his way back from Russia.) I walked across the stage questioning reality and mentally shaking my head. A tall balding Admiral smiled and pinned on my coveted Naval Aviator's wings. I still had no handle on what I had accomplished; didn't have any idea of what was next.

As Naval Aviation Cadets, this graduation not only meant we were at last—fully qualified pilots, but (somehow) also qualified to be Commissioned Officers. This appointment involved a signature for each one of us, by the President of United States (who at least in my case had no earthly idea of my qualifications). *A cadet yesterday and an Officer today*. Ensign is the entry rank for a Commissioned Officer in the Navy. But there was another option. After eighteen months as a Navy cadet, if one graduated in the top ten percent of his class and favorably impressed a stern-faced board of leatherneck officers, he could choose to be commissioned as a Second Lieutenant in the Marine Corps! I had undoubtedly been lucky again, and did so! That's it for my Naval Aviator Training—from start to finish. A not remarkable set of memories I admit, but those they are. I was finished. I'd done it.

CHAPTER TWENTY-NINE
On My Own At Last

For any new Marine pilot, the choice duty station upon graduation was El Toro Marine Corps Air Station, in Santa Ana, California (just thirty minutes from Hollywood) *and I got it!* There were movie stars, health nuts, sports cars, cool surfing dudes, and most importantly, an eyeful of tanned, hard-bodied, honey-haired females wherever you looked. It was everything and more recanted in the familiar lyrics of the *Beach Boys'* songs. It was just about everything a young bachelor could possibly dream of. This would be my best chance yet to break out.

And I was not totally among strangers sampling the Southern Cal good life. Several of my best flight training buddies, including Jack Pulcheon (the "Animal") and Allan Yatsko my Texas Preflight roommate, had also gotten El Toro. The Animal was assigned to my squadron while Allan went to a historic WWII fighter squadron.

My new squadron VMCJ-3 was an Electro-Countermeasures and Aerial Photography squadron, jokingly referred to as the "Gentlemen's Squadron." With only a reconnaissance mission our aircraft did not have guns nor could they carry rockets or bombs. (We were the brunt of comments about the "kinder, gentler" aspect of Marine aviation.) Many of the senior officers had actually flown in World War II, and of course all of them had flown in the Korean conflict. Back then we were not fighting segments of the civilian population in an attempt to "keep some third world government in power." We were fighting enemies that had attacked one of our allies (and unlike our present conflicts, our opponents actually had uniformed armies and air forces with operative aircraft to confront our planes!) The Animal and I listened attentively anytime the live combat stories got going.

The squadron had two types of aircraft. One was a hugely engined propeller-driven aircraft: the AD-5N *Sky Raider*. During the Korean conflict and even Vietnam it had been an attack and close air support aircraft (dropping bombs and shooting rockets). Now, ours were modified for a different mission. It had specialized electronic equipment installed, allowing it to find enemy radar sites and pin-point the locations. The second type aircraft was a swept wing jet—the F9F-8 *Cougar*. It was a photo-capability version of the famous F9F-5 *Panther* that Harry Brubaker flew in the classic William Holden film, *The Bridges of Toko Ri*. Using it to take aerial photos required very precise flying. You had to maintain an absolutely non-varying heading and altitude (not only to stay on the target, but to keep the cameras at the right focal length). Animal and I would begin making almost-daily flights in each of these type aircraft, perfecting our skills in both electro-countermeasures and aerial photography. This preparatory phase in the life cycle of a tactical Marine squadron is called Phase One and lasts twelve months. Phase Two is the tactical phase, which in our case would be an overseas deployment to Japan. There, we would do the same type flying, except now we would do it for real, up and down the coast of the Soviet Union.

In addition to flying duties each young officer was assigned a collateral duty. Animal was the Assistant Maintenance Officer. I was assigned as the Survival Officer, which meant I gave weekly presentations on ways to survive a crash at sea or some remote land location, and sustain oneself till rescued. During one such presentation I was explaining the proper use of the Signal Mirror, a thick 4X6 inch sized mirror with a see-thru aiming sight in the middle. A downed airman could aim it so as to reflect the sun's rays into the cockpit of the Search and Rescue plane. The hope was that the bright flashes into the eyes of the rescue plane pilot would pinpoint the downed airman's position, which might otherwise be hard to see. A pilot dangling in his parachute in a thick jungle canopy would never be seen, and a small yellow raft is hard to find in a hundred square miles of ocean. I advised the group that since the mirror was not simple to use, they should read the "Instructions for Use" printed on the rear side of it in advance, *in case they needed to use it at night.* You might imagine, this statement resulted in a chorus of guffaws.

Not feeling ready to live on the economy (off-base) I opted to live in the "BOQ" (Bachelor Officers' Quarters) on base. It was a lot like a college dorm, minus the fact that it was almost empty. Most single guys opted for a bachelor's pad in the nearby town of Laguna Beach. At twenty-one I had not yet had an apartment or lived alone, so postponed this residency off base. However, from time to time I was invited to dinner at one of my braver cohort's cool digs on the beach.

On the way back to the base from one such late evening, I stopped at a local diner for a piece of pie and a cup of coffee. Just finishing the pie, the entrance door swung open and in walked what had to be a "lady of the night." She must have been mid shift; open blouse, bra showing, short tight skirt wrinkled and twisted off center, tousled dyed red hair, with badly smudged lipstick and mascara. Whew! And evidently she had allowed an assortment of papers and receipts to accumulate on the front seat of her car, because—you know those adhesive-backed *Green Stamps* that the grocery stores used to give out for sizable purchases, to encourage a patron to buy again? As she passed my booth I saw a whole sheet of them stuck to her backside.

After only a few months at El Toro, still decompressing from the previous 18 months of flight training, I was early on in the experiment of living an independent single life; not yet having been responsible for a residence, and in no position to be qualified to even consider moving on to any next phase, *it's hard to believe a too early commitment I let myself in for*. Occasionally one of my married friends living off base would invite me over to sample that lifestyle. Allan Yatsko and his lovely wife Caroline invited me to dinner at their stilted wood home, perched on a cliff overlooking one of Laguna Beach's most beautiful hidden coves. Here they had a life that I felt they deserved and could only be envied; one beautiful, stress-free day after another, with only a two-minute descent down to their own personal beach. She the happy stay-at-home wife and he the swaggering "top gun" of what used to be Pappy Boyington's *Black Sheep* squadron (and later popularized in a made for TV series).

Along with me they had invited Tom Blune, a fellow Marine we had both known in flight training. Prior to entering the Naval Cadet program Tom had been the starting quarterback for the University of Missouri. He was a sturdy, fireplug guy, with freckles and close-cropped red hair. To initial appearances, he was quiet spoken and polite, but not someone to be challenged—especially physically. He could be fiercely aggressive. The most popular hang out in Laguna Beach was the famous Sandpiper bar right on the coast highway. One night a hulking rowdy civilian got into a row with Tom (which happened often) and invited Tom outside. Big mistake. In less than a minute the giant had been hit a dozen times and was crumpled on the sidewalk. And a couple months ago all three of us had been sent to an Escape and Evasion course in the mountains of northern California. There, enlisted Marines dressed as enemy soldiers would capture us, confine us, and interrogate us. (Realistic training to see if we could stick to the "name, rank and serial number" only). Tom escaped every time, in fact once breaking the jaw of one corporal assigned as a guard. Don't think he planned on making the military a career; told us his uncle in St. Louis was going to retire and give him his entire dental practice. I couldn't much picture Tom as a dentist; nor could anyone, and he would not become one. (Much more on him later.)

As usual Tom would be there with his fiancée—an absolutely knock-out gorgeous local girl. Up till tonight I had never seen Valerie not in a bikini. And I hate to admit it—a bikini that was never quite up to the task of confining or covering so many luscious areas anxious to escape. Tonight she was dressed in a lavender tank top and white cotton shorts which seemed to be lifting her off the ground. (If I stole a glance at her crotch area, it made me feel as if I should give a tug down on the hem of my own boxer shorts.)

The evening went swell—couldn't have been better. Caroline made a terrific Italian dinner. A good time was being had by all (helped along by one delicious innards-warming glass of wine after another). Caroline would leap to her feet at any request from Allan, accomplish the mission and return to the table with a big and loving smile. And Tom and Valerie while continuing to finalize the plans for their October wedding were obviously getting along just fine as well. Could hardly keep my eyes off Valerie, sitting on his lap with her shapely tan arms around his neck and proud breasts pressed against him. She never let more than thirty seconds pass without planting another long kiss.

By the end of the meal the room was aglow and full of contented smiles (and the sink was full of empty Chianti bottles). The world was a wonderful place to be. I was favorably impressed by this married and "about-to-be-married" lifestyle. It was my first observance of it among my peers. This evening would have convinced anyone that it was something to be highly sought after. In the midst of this warm conjecture I realized Caroline was speaking to me. "And Roger, how about you, you must have a girlfriend somewhere."

Had to think. No one came to mind (understandably). But then, "Yes, yes I do." I began to tell her about Sara, a girl I had met at a church summer camp back in high school, and during flight training had written to her once or twice. In fact, on one home leave I went out on a movie date with her (mainly because she was the only girl I knew). They all chimed in with "tell us more" and "so what's happening now." I obliged, for some reason elevating all aspects of the relationship. Between sips of an after dinner Mexican liqueur (that Allan had personally bought in Reynosa and insisted we try) I continued to embellish (or manufacture) my new girlfriend's admirable traits, her attractiveness, her honesty, her family values, and her "true-to-me-only" qualities. The other four were all ears. I heard the at best casual link between Sara and me turning into something a lot more serious; getting better and better and more and more conclusive.

Can't remember who suggested it or why in the hell I went along with it, but after some minutes of this escalating dialogue, I had been directed to the phone and was dialing Information for Sara's number. I don't recollect any details of the conversation, but when it was over I was being roundly toasted and slapped on the back. Evidently I had somehow said or at least allowed Sara to conclude that I was not just calling to rekindle a relationship, but was more or less suggesting it was sufficiently advanced that we might even get engaged! The shocking, larger than life, unanticipated result of the call: Only a few months later *a diamond ring would be in the mail.*

CHAPTER THIRTY
A NOT GOOD Happening, Again

Once again, not just things of mass, but ideas and situations can have an inertia—a momentum of their own. Similar to the succession of seemingly destined or automated responses that led to my college enrollment, and then the fortuitous progression through flight training, another even more crucial event materialized just three months later. In December 1957—two months after my twenty-second birthday, *I became a married man!* This without having gone steady with or even spent any quality time (let alone an overnight) with my wife-to-be. I'm not sure what being in love feels like, or if it's necessary. My only semblance was my relationship with Connie. Now *married?* An act in retrospect that I was definitely not ready or qualified for. I knew nothing of myself, or my possible place in the world. Not thinking ahead again. I hadn't considered the first real thing about what being married would mean; had no idea of what it would put an end to—its consummate commitment and permanence!

My second thoughts were not long in coming—hitting me about ten minutes after the ceremony. I say this because even years later, looking at the last photo in our wedding album (that one taken from behind the getaway car—through the rear window) where the bride and groom are smiling over their shoulder to the photographer. It was not hard to see the befuddlement in my eyes; a frightful *"what on earth have I just done"* look in them.

The wedding was held in Sara's church back in Jersey. To save the cross-country airfare getting there, I hitched a ride on a military aircraft. Animal drove me to a northern California military base to bum a flight to the east coast. While I was able to catch a flight and pull it off, it was not a comfortable trip. I rode (freezing) in the clear plastic paneled nose gunner's cone of an old WWII Navy patrol bomber. The aircraft had strange (or imagined) engine problems, causing the captain to stop three times on the way to the east coast! I thought Naval Air Station Philadelphia—a three-hour drive from home, would have been close enough. Perhaps because of being six hours late and then arriving at 2 a.m., it was clear Dad was not all happy.

There were a couple of family get-togethers, two or three rehearsals, and then the wedding. A wonderful old-fashioned eastern European wedding. Everything went smoothly. No drunks. No fights. No relatives pulling you into a corner for lengthy counsel. During the reception I observed a traditional event from the old country: *The dance with the bride.* Any male (regardless of age) who wanted to dance with the bride, had to put whatever money he could afford into a hat to do so. There wasn't a man or boy present who did not avail himself of this opportunity. You should have seen the loot we pulled in!

There was one memorable but embarrassing occurrence at the reception. Sara's immigrant parents had arrived in the United States from Canada, and many of her relatives in attendance still lived there. Sara arranged a greeting line so she could introduce me to all her uncles and aunts from Canada. In an attempt to appear more quick-witted, I endeavored to greet each one with a different salutation: "Pleased to meet you." "How are you today." "Thank you so much for making the trip." "My pleasure indeed."

Well after the fifth or sixth new greeting I was scratching the bottom of the barrel. A dapper man in a gold-buttoned, double-breasted blazer was in front of me when I thought of a new one and blurted it out: "Hi, I've heard a lot about you." *The place went dead.* You could have heard a pin drop. Later Sara informed me: That uncle had recently left his wife and run away with his secretary.

My folks' wedding gift to us was the airline ticket for Sara and me back to Los Angeles (albeit on a serious "red eye" flight). We spent some time in the terminal counting the ones, fives, and even tens received from *the dance with the bride.* (This was 1957—a ten would be equivalent to a lot more now!) We heard the call for our midnight boarding and stuffed all the loot into our carry-on. During one of the delays while taxiing out to the runway, Sara commented that she had not even felt us go airborne. I explained why.

Got into LA about seven a.m. Retrieved all the bags okay. Navigated the huge parking lot complex without a problem and found the T-Bird precisely where Animal said he had left it. It was a fun drive south to Laguna Beach. This was Sara's first trip to California (if not her first time out of New Jersey) and she was awed by typical L.A. sights. "Roger! That car is *pink*!" "Wow, look at that *crazy* palm tree!" "That person is walking *four* dogs!" "Roger that woman is wearing *orange stretch pants* and she's eighty if she's a day!"

Regarding our first marital digs, I had been really lucky. A buddy tipped me off to a great rental coming available. It was a cute, multi-colored cottage designed and built by some Swedish guy. Soon as I saw it I signed a rental agreement. The real estate agent told me it had been featured in *Better Homes and Gardens*. And it was (the cover page from that article framed and mounted on the wall just inside the door). Sara was mightily impressed. The house was located high in the hills just east of the famous coast highway; in an exclusive area of Laguna Beach known as *Top of the World*. Many of these homes have since been destroyed by wildfires, or as a result of heavy rains had the earth beneath them give way, causing them to cascade into the ravines below.

I was a little nervous as the sun began to set on our first day of life together, knowing we would soon be spending the first *night* of our life together; joining our bodies for the first time. During the afternoon we unpacked and put clothes away, rearranged some furniture, did grocery shopping, and paid a short visit to Allan and Caroline. In the evening we tried to make it seem old shoe by making small talk and watching some TV. (I think both of us delaying just a bit, aware of the scope of the forthcoming event.) But now it was after ten and in view of the day we'd had, neither of us could think of a reason to stay up longer. I was already in my recently purchased silk boxer shorts. Sara got her night gown and went to the bathroom to ready herself. I passed the time stretched out on the batik print couch in the living room (feigning relaxing, when in truth I was tight as a drum, shivering if I relaxed). She was out all too soon. I met her in as romantic a way as I knew how, kissing her forehead, putting one arm around her waist and taking her hand. I escorted her into the bedroom and to the huge platform bed (which had been brought over from Sweden). The solid side walls were three and a half feet high and adorned with hand painted Scandinavian winter scenes. I helped her up the few steps of the attached ladder and then joined her under the sheets.

I lay still for a while, so as not to appear too anxious (and to get my thoughts together). When it seemed appropriate I raised up, leaned over, and kissed her tenderly, and then gently began what I hoped would be a pleasurable foreplay for her. I continued, not rushing, and found it this time to be pleasurable to me as well. This was my wife—clean, sweet, innocent; ready to give herself to me. *It was going to be a wonderful physical and spiritual union.* After a reasonable time of stroking and kissing, I became concerned as once again I didn't feel the beginnings of an arousal; not yet close to being in possession of what would be necessary. Sara lay there quiet and wonderfully patient (and thankfully refraining from giving me instructions or encouragement). I did this and I did that, but I didn't do "it." In spite of several awkwardly futile attempts to do so, I was unable to enter her (hoping her inexperience would keep her from realizing my problem). But she did. I was enormously embarrassed and discouraged. Sara was very supportive and thankfully had heard from some unknown great friend of mine, about this possible non-occurrence. Lying there after all had been abandoned, she reassured me that this was not at all uncommon, and not to worry.

But of course I *was* worried! I certainly had not forgotten my fateful late-night experience with Connie. For the first time I was fearful that at least in my case (now with an O for 2 track record) it might not be so uncommon. All through high school the mere sight (or thought) of the inside of a woman's thigh would produce a prompt and embarrassing response. The end-of-period bell would often find me sneaking out of class holding a notebook in front of my pelvis to hide an uninvited protrusion. Hope against hope! I knew there would be other nights and was just praying this deficiency—striking me now, was because sadly, both Connie and my wife just did not have the right chemistry; what I needed. And that it would not be something that would turn my life into who knows what kind of life.

Epilogue

I Guess I Just Wasn't Thinking continues

Part Two: The French Riviera, Leo, June, and Big Trouble: Get ready to find yourself in the middle of a gripping, suspense-filled, scarcely credible saga; one carried out in the midst of a moving and meaningful global search for a solution that may not exist, and the commencement of a shocking new life for Roger. We again meet him, but now as a young Marine captain assigned as an attack pilot aboard a Supercarrier in the Mediterranean. The reader will gain a new respect (or frightening concern) for the military component of our foreign policy. He has his own nuclear weapon and his own target: a small city in Romania which he will vaporize, should the Russians launch one ballistic missile westward. (Or the scary part: should someone somewhere, monitoring a scope, mistakenly *think* they did.) There are ample accounts of white-knuckle flight operations as well as both mirthful and tragic events aboard ship. *But that's not the half of it!*

The search begins! Part One ended with Roger discovering or confirming the presence of—if permanent, a devastating deficiency; a potential truly life-altering condition. While his wonderful wife had not seemed overly distressed by his incapacity, he is cruelly tormented by it 24/7. He never ruminates that he may have a physiological problem; concluding instead that *Connie and his wife just did not have the right chemistry.* He clings to the hope that the one woman with it, who will unlock his manhood is out there somewhere, possibly waiting for him in one of the storied European cities or jet set haunts the ship's crew will explore. He is amazed his mediocrity is not seen, and while lacking the stature and elan it should take he meets rogues and royalty. The reader may feel that the heart-stopping aviation activities take a back seat to the chance, flamboyance, and shame of Roger's exploits ashore.